PETER CORRIS is known as the 'godfather' of Australian crime fiction through his Cliff Hardy detective stories. He has written in many other areas, including a co-authored autobiography of the late Professor Fred Hollows, a history of boxing in Australia, spy novels, historical novels and a collection of short stories about golf (see www.petercorris. net). In 2009, Peter Corris was awarded the Ned Kelly Award for Best Fiction by the Crime Writers Association of Australia. He is married to writer Jean Bedford and has lived in Sydney for most of his life. They have three daughters and six grandsons.

The Cliff Hardy collection

PETER
CORRIS

BURN, AND OTHER STORIES

ALLEN&UNWIN
SYDNEY • MELBOURNE • AUCKLAND • LONDON

This edition published by Allen & Unwin in 2014
First published by Bantam Books, a division of Transworld Publishers, in 1993

Allen & Unwin
83 Alexander Street
Crows Nest NSW 2065
Australia
Phone: (61 2) 8425 0100
Email: info@allenandunwin.com
Web: www.allenandunwin.com

Cataloguing-in-Publication details are available
from the National Library of Australia
www.trove.nla.gov.au

ISBN 978 1 76011 016 1 (pbk)
ISBN 978 1 74343 798 8 (ebook)

Printed and bound in Australia by Griffin Press

MIX
Paper from
responsible sources
FSC
www.fsc.org   FSC® C009448

The paper in this book is FSC certified.
FSC promotes environmentally responsible,
socially beneficial and economically viable
management of the world's forests.

For Steve Wright and Marian Macgowan

Several of the stories in this collection have been previously published in slightly different versions as follows: 'Burn' in the *Bulletin* December 1988; 'The House of Ruby' in *Mean Streets* 1, 1991; 'Lost and Found' in *SPAN* 31, 1991: 'Cadigal Country' in *Homeland* ed. George Papaellinas, Allen & Unwin 1991; 'The Big Lie' in *More Crimes for a Summer Christmas* ed. Stephen Knight, Allen & Unwin 1991; and 'Ghost Writer' in *A Corpse at the Opera House* ed. Stephen Knight, Allen & Unwin 1992.

Several of the stories in this collection have been
previously published in slightly different versions
as follows: 'Burn' in the Bulletin December 1988,
'The House of Rory' in short shorts 1, 1991, 'Loss'
and 'Found' in SCOPE AH 199? 'Coastal County'
in Townsville 64 percent Pagesetting, where a
Linocut 1990, 'The big List' in Story Cows for
a Saturday Christmas at Spirhen Knight, After
Ts Dawng 1991 and 'Cancer Writes' in a Cosque
Bride Opera House and Stephen Knight, After a
Linocut 1992.

Contents

Contents

Burn

'Mr Hardy, I can't believe he did it, not Jason. George? Sure, all the bloody time. But not Jason.'

'He's run away,' I said. 'Doesn't mean he's guilty necessarily, but it doesn't help.'

Mavis Wishart looked around my office with its faded walls and battered furniture. And this is my *new* office, down the hall from the old one which kind of died after a shotgun went off in it, several times. Mavis was comfortable here; you could tell she'd seen plenty of faded walls in her time. She was a small, dark woman of around forty, possibly part Aboriginal or Islander, but she looked as if she'd been too busy all her life to notice. She'd raised two sons without either father to help. Now the younger son was accused of setting fire to his school. He'd run away and she wanted me to find him.

I looked at the notes I'd made. 'Thirteen, fourteen next month. 175 centimetres. That's tall for thirteen.'

Mavis shrugged. 'His father was tall.'

'Nearly fourteen, isn't that a bit old for sixth class?'

'His father was dumb.' Mavis grinned as she spoke. 'Nah, he's not dumb. Jase missed a lot of school early, so did George. We moved around a lot and they were always sick.'

'The fire was ten days ago. You saw him that night and not since.'

'Right. The cops were round in the morning, I went up to get Jase out of bed, but he must have heard them coming. The window was open and he was gone. Look, Mr Hardy, Jason's a good kid, but you know how things are these days. A push in the wrong direction and they're gone. Ma Parker told me you'd got her Annie out of trouble once.'*

'Once,' I said. 'It didn't work out so well in the end.'

'Have a shot at this,' Mavis said. 'It might turn out better. His brother, George, burnt down three schools. That's why the cops came after Jase.'

She was a game, good-humoured woman, so I took the case. Mavis wrote me a cheque for $300— two days, maybe three at my soft-boiled rate. I had a description of the kid, names and addresses of his mates and the location of the pinball joints and pubs he frequented; this was Sydney's inner west, and Jason Wishart was nearly fourteen after all.

I spent two days on it, then a third day. I checked on the other kids and the hangouts. With runaways,

* see *Heroin Annie* (1984) and *Man in the Shadows* (1988)

2

usually, that's all it takes—they're either in the near neighbourhood or they're long gone. When the names and addresses yielded nothing, I tried the institutions. The patience of Detective Sergeant Hubbard of the Darlington police station was stretched to breaking point by a hundred different frustrations, but he gave me the time of day. He admitted that he'd had a tip-off about Jason Wishart after the fire at the local primary school.

'When?' I said.

'That night.'

'Isn't that a bit quick?'

Hubbard sighed and blinked tired eyes. I could guess at the relationship between the eyes and the piles of paper on his desk. 'Look, Hardy, if you knew someone was screwing your wife and you got a tip it was me, what would you do?'

'I might make a mental note that she'd dropped her standards. My wife left me years ago. Are you trying to be offensive?'

'I'm trying to get you to piss off. Georgie Wishart torched schools around here like they were named Guy Fawkes Primary. I'm told he's in the Navy now. God help them. His brother was and is the chief suspect.'

If that took me into ancient history, the talk with the headmistress of the school took me into politics. Clarissa Fielding was large, grey-haired and imposing. 'The fire didn't help,' she said. 'The school's under threat of closing. I doubt if we'll get the money to fix the damage.'

3

I sat in her office, which looked as if it had doubled as a storeroom, and gazed out at the kids playing in the school grounds—if you could call a couple of hundred square metres of unshaded asphalt that. 'Closing? Why?'

'Declining numbers.' Mrs Fielding waved an ironical hand at the window. A ball bounced off the glass as if underlining her point.

'Looks busy to me.'

'It's nonsense. All the projections are that in two years' time this area will have more children than it had five years ago.'

'Ah,' I murmured, 'rationalisation.'

Mrs Fielding snorted. 'Exploitation. The plan is to sell the closed schools. This site is worth millions to the developers and, believe me, they know it.'

I was about to ask more questions but she forestalled me by standing up. 'If you're really interested, Mr Hardy, you can come to one of the protest meetings. They're widely advertised. I'm afraid I can't help you about Jason Wishart. His attendance wasn't good. His teachers' reports suggest he could have done better.'

I stood, too. 'They always say that. They said that about me.'

'I expect they were right.'

I left the school by the west gate. I could hear the roar of the Cleveland Street traffic but the area was gentrifying nevertheless. I looked back at the old building—most likely it'd be flattened in favour of townhouses or office blocks plus parking. A woman standing by the gate thrust a pamphlet into my hand.

'Save our school.'

'Hear, hear,' I said.

I glanced at the pamphlet which called for a halt to the selling of school sites and named developers and real estate agents who'd expressed 'unseemly interest in our school'. I put the paper in my pocket.

It was pretty much blank wall time, but I decided to pay a call on Jason Wishart's brother, although everyone told me that the Wishart boys weren't close. George Wishart shared a flat in Marrickville with two other sailors. His mother had told me that he was on shore leave.

'Not that he'll bother to come and see me.'

The red brick block was small and the flats had no view, but I suppose if you're at sea most of the time, you can do without views on land. The hungover, fair, fattish young man who answered my knock looked nothing like Mavis or the dark whippet of a boy that was Jason in the photo she had given me.

'I'm looking for George Wishart.'

'Why?'

That reply told me I'd found him. People are incurious on the whole. 'Your mother gave me your address. Your brother's in trouble.'

'Too bad.' He tried to close the door but maybe he was used to bulkheads. I had my foot in the gap and my shoulder pushing against him before he could get set. I shoved the door in and he almost lost balance.

'Hey,' he yelped, 'this is a break-in.'

'Don't be silly.' His fat, vacant face annoyed me. I was also feeling frustrated by the inquiry. That's a bad combination in my game—meeting someone uncongenial when frustrated. I brushed him aside and looked quickly through the flat: the place was a shit-hole—dirty beds, floors, tables, and a kitchen that was a health hazard.

George was sitting on the arm of a chair smoking a cigarette when I came back into the living room.

'You didn't look in the dunny,' he said.

'It's all a dunny. When did you last see Jason?'

His eyes flickered to the telephone standing on top of a pile of current and out-of-date directories. 'Months ago. Who're you?'

'Captain Bligh. He was here, wasn't he? What did he want—money?'

'I wouldn't give the little . . .'

George was smart enough to see that he'd made a mistake. He flicked ash on the floor. 'He was in his bloody pyjamas. He wanted to make a phone call. I let him and then I told him to piss off.'

'Brotherly love. Who did he call?'

'I dunno. STD. He had the number in his head, then he wrote it down in the book and rang it.'

I picked up the directories and thumbed through them. Numbers were scribbled at random in the margins and over the type. The only STD number was written in a childish pencil scrawl on the inside flap of the A-K volume—the prefix was 045.

I read it out. 'This it?'

George shrugged and flicked more ash. I wrote the number in my notebook. 'Did Jason say anything to you about setting fire to a school?'

George sneered. 'He wouldn't have the guts.'

'Did you tell this to the police?'

Alarm flared in George's bloodshot eyes. 'I wasn't here when they came.'

I went past him, closing my nostrils against his frowsy, sweaty stink. 'Why don't you have a shave and a shower and go and see your mother.'

'Why?' he said.

You can trace names from telephone numbers if you've got the right connections. I put through a call and got the information I needed. I knew from the prefix that the service was to the Richmond district—the subscriber was Mark Scammell of Lot 1, Brewer's Lagoon Road, Richmond. If I hadn't encountered the SOS woman at the school gate an hour earlier, the name wouldn't have meant a thing to me. I dug the pamphlet from my pocket and confirmed my recollection that Scammell was named as one of the property developers intensely interested in the asphalt and bricks the Education Department was putting up for sale.

It was mid-afternoon and warm. Driving west for a couple of hours would be no fun, but following a strong scent is fun in itself. I went home, showered and changed and did some quick research on Scammell. He operated two real estate agencies in Sydney, one in the Blue Mountains, another on the south coast, and was the managing director of Atlas Properties Inc.

The sun was low in the sky when I set off. I stopped at a service station for petrol, a detailed map of Richmond and the paper. The headline was: ANOTHER SCHOOL GOES UP IN SMOKE! The sketchy report said that an inner west infants' school had been severely damaged by a fire which bore resemblances to the one thirteen days previously. I put the paper in the glovebox on top of my .38 Smith & Wesson and headed for the Hawkesbury.

City people hide in the country and country people hide in the city. Who said that? Maybe I did. Anyway, I'd played enough big-time hide-and-seek to believe that it was true. The commuter traffic, with its share of Brocks and Gardiners, kept me from thinking much about the connection between Scammell and the kid until I reached Blacktown. After that, on the Windsor Road, it should have been easier to think but a succession of trucks interrupted the process. Result was, I reached Richmond as the last of the daylight died, and located Brewer's Lagoon Road without doing any significant analysis or planning. What the hell. As Jack Dempsey said, 'Don't think, punch.'

I pulled off the road and into a dip about a hundred metres from the house lights. There were never going to be a lot of lots in Brewer's Lagoon Road. In fact, indications were that Scammell's place was the whole story. Mark seemed to have found himself a couple of acres wedged in between Commonwealth land, an agricultural college and a bit of national park. He had a lake about a good tee shot from his oiled teak front door and a river view from the brick patio at the back. Toss in a lot of grass, a tennis court, pool and three-car garage and you have some idea of the place.

I put the gun in one jacket pocket, the keys in the other, opened and closed the car door softly and moved towards the house. The nearest lights from other houses were a long way off. I picked up a solid bit of wood as a dog persuader and began a careful perusal of the waist-high drystone fence that ran along the eastern border of the property. When I was sure it wasn't wired or sensored, I climbed over it. I steered clear of the gravel driveway and the lights that picked out attractive features of the garden and aimed for the steps that led up to the patio. Patios have glass windows that are often left open and have crummy locks anyway. You can look through them, slide them open or break in, whatever.

The patio and the back of the house were dark. I picked the lock on the glass door and slipped into a room big enough to play touch football in. The hallway was wide and short. I nipped down it towards the front of the house where I could hear voices.

A woman said, 'You wouldn't dare say that if Ralph was here.'

A man said, 'I would.'

I crept into a huge tiled kitchen. There was a serving hatch in one wall and I peeked through it into a big room with chairs and couches on a deep pile carpet square with polished wood surrounds. A stereo with about a hundred compact discs in a rack stood beside heavy drapes covering a window, and there was a TV set with a screen the size of a bedsheet. The voices were coming from the TV's hi-fi speakers. Jason Wishart was sprawled in a chair sucking on a can of Fosters. Three crumpled cans lay on the floor beside him. A man sat opposite him watching the TV.

Suddenly, Wishart moved his hand and the screen went blank.

'Fuck you! I was watching that!' The man moved smoothly across the room. He belted the boy in the face and swooped on the remote control. Wishart tried to lever himself up, but he got a jab in the ribs and sank back.

'I want to get out of here, Brian.'

'When he says so, not until. Relax and watch the show. Have another beer.' The screen came alive again. 'I'll keep the remote. You don't seem to know how to use it.'

I waited until the talking heads had got back into affirming and denying things before I came up behind Brian. He was a tall, skinny type with thinning hair brushed back. With the muzzle of the .38, I tapped him on the head where the scalp was showing through.

'Put your hands up there, Brian, and cover your bald spot.'

He pitched forward into a dive roll, twisted as he came out of it and somehow pulled a gun. He got off one shot which went high and wide. I went down behind the chair.

'This is crazy,' I yelled. I sneaked a look around the chair. Maybe Brian *was* crazy—he was certainly trying to line up another shot. I braced myself and rushed at him, using the chair as a battering ram and shield. Brian fired again but missed by an even wider margin. The chair hit him in the knees and shins and he went over. I gave him another jolt with the chair before I left its cover. He'd dropped his gun and was scrabbling for it so I kicked it across the carpet into the corner of the room.

Brian was keen. He came up off the floor like a thin lion after a fat Christian. I sidestepped and tripped him as he went past. He cannoned into a stand that held a five-litre bottle of Johnny Walker scotch. The bottle hit the wall and broke and the room suddenly smelt like a distillery. I was getting set to issue orders when Jason Wishart picked up a box of matches from the floor, struck one and tossed it onto the scotch-soaked carpet. A sheet of flame leapt up and enveloped the heavy drapes across the windows. The fire licked at the oiled and polished woodwork, caught and jumped to the over-stuffed furniture and racks of compact discs. Bits of flaming plastic spat out around the room.

I rushed at Wishart, hit him low and let him collapse onto my shoulder. I took him towards the door in a fireman's lift.

'Extinguisher? Where's the fuckin' extinguisher?' Brian yelled.

He was mobile and had enough breath to shout so I left him to it. I went out through the kitchen, across the patio and down onto the grass. Wishart couldn't have weighed much more than forty-five kilos and in my adrenalin-rushed state he was no burden. I made it to my car and folded him into the front seat. I took a look back at the house before I drove off—Brian needed more than an extinguisher now, he needed four brigades. The place was burning like Dresden.

I got the story from young Wishart as he sobered up on the drive back to Sydney. He hadn't torched the school, but he had been in trouble earlier as a member of a graffiti gang that had broken into one of Scammell's properties and caused some damage. Scammell's security men had caught Wishart but Scammell had let him go.

'He was real nice to me. Helped me out a few times.'

I asked him why he was getting into trouble in the first place.

'I found out one of my grandads was a Maori. I'm confused.'

'Both my grandmas were Irish,' I said. 'Imagine how I feel.'

Scammell had given Wishart his number with an instruction to call him if he needed help. Wishart had done so after the cops came looking for him. He'd been held against his will in Richmond ever since.

'He was setting you up as the Number One school arsonist. Probably would've dumped you in the lake eventually. The fires'd help to close down the schools. Big bucks for the developer— Scammell.'

Wishart stroked the dark down on his upper lip and stared through the windscreen at the empty road. 'That's a real downer,' he said.

I delivered him back to his mother and sat in on a conference between them and Hubbard, the unsympathetic cop, the next day. Hubbard grunted, took notes and went away.

'What now?' Mavis Wishart said.

'With luck,' I said, 'nothing.'

I heard from police sources that Mark Scammell went interstate the night his Richmond villa burned down, and overseas shortly after that. No charges were brought in respect of the school fires and last I heard Jason Wishart's school was still func-tioning while the SOS group fought the govern-ment's closure plans.

I kept digging a little in my spare time and when

Scammell got back to Sydney in December I made an appointment to see him, saying that I was interested in selling my house in Glebe. No real estate agent could ignore that. He was a big, fleshy man with close-set, shrewd eyes.

'What's your equity?' he said.

I leaned back in the leather chair. 'Bad luck about your place in Richmond,' I said. 'Big loss.'

The shrewd eyes went hostile. 'Insurance'll cover it. Now . . .'

'How about the clause that cancels the insurance if a criminal act is involved.'

'What?'

'I was there,' I said. 'Brian took a shot at me. I made a statement to the police. I can make one to your insurance company. You won't get a bean.'

Scammell's loose, floppy mouth tightened. 'What do you want?'

'I thought a cheque made out to SOS.'

'No way.'

'I had a little talk with Brian last week. He's not too happy with you, leaving the country like that.'

Scammell slid open a drawer and took out a chequebook.

'Make it $10,000,' I said, 'and write it big and clear. I've got a photographer and a reporter downstairs. They might want a close-up of the cheque.'

Eye Doctor

'An eye doctor?' I said. 'I had some dealings with one once a little while back. Mind you, I didn't see much of him, especially when he was operating on me.'

'You always liked your little joke, Cliff,' Ian Sangster said. 'But this is important. Could you be serious for a minute?'

'Sure,' I said, but I couldn't help myself, I was in such a good mood. 'I also knew an undertaker, but he's dead.'

I burst out laughing. Dr Ian Sangster looked at me the way he might at a victim of brain damage. 'Am I going to have to give you something to calm you down? What're you on? I've probably got the antidote.'

'Glen and I are going up to her place on the coast next week. We're going to catch fish and swim and rub oil all over each other, day and night.'

'When next week?'

'Friday.'

'Good. Ten days away. That'll give you time

to do this job. It'll pay well, not that you need much money for what you've got planned. Mind you, if it comes to rings . . .'

I held up my hand. 'Don't be ridiculous. Money wouldn't hurt, but I couldn't take any from you.'

Sangster has been my doctor for most of the last twenty years. He's patched me and other people up at unlikely hours and in unlikely places, and provided other extracurricular services. He hasn't filed reports or charged the going rates. Now, he pushed aside his scotch and leaned forward—two signs that he really was serious.

'It's not for me. It's for Jonas Buckawa. You've heard of him, haven't you?'

I had. Buckawa was a Bougainvillean lawyer and politician who was holding up the works in a big way. A major petroleum strike had been made in the strait between the islands of Buka and Bougainville and financial interests in Papua New Guinea, Australia and Singapore were falling over themselves to get the drills down and the barrels filling. Buckawa had found a dozen different objections to the contracts—in terms of the environment, traditional ownership and usage of the waters, the terms decided between the contracting parties and their governments—as well as doubts about the reliability of the survey work estimate of the reserves. He'd filed his objections in a series of courts, including the International Court, and he'd got the media interested and the locals stirred up so that the prospective field was

16

constantly under surveillance. The PNG government wanted to send in troops. Singapore, it was said, supported that; Australia could not.

'What's his problem?' I said. 'He seems to have the ball at his feet.'

'He does, in a sense. He stands a good chance of winning his court battles and bringing a stop to all this oil-drilling bullshit.'

Ian is a conservationist, worried about greenhouse gases, the ozone layer, pollution, everything. I tried to think of when I'd last read anything about Buckawa and realised that it had been some time. I'd assumed it was just a matter of legal wheels turning slowly. Evidently not.

'Jonas has had severe eye trouble for some time—cataracts and glaucoma. It's got worse. He needs an operation, a tricky one. It has to be kept secret though. If word got out that he has these problems the campaign'd collapse, it's all on his shoulders. That's where Professor Frank Harkness comes in. He's worked in Bougainville, Jonas knows and trusts him. He can do the job and keep his mouth shut. He's a bit of a stirrer himself.'

'Is that right?' I was sceptical. I didn't associate eye surgeons with much except clever hands and big bank accounts. 'I still don't see why you need me.'

'We—I'm on the Buka Strait Committee—need someone to protect Harkness. Jonas is getting into Sydney the day after tomorrow, very much on the quiet, illegally in fact. The PNG government took

17

away his passport. We've got people to look after him but the same sort of people can't be seen to be hanging around Harkness.'

'Bougainvilleans, you mean?'

Ian nodded. 'Not everyone up there's on side, not by a long shot. If someone unsympathetic in Sydney spotted odd comings and goings around Harkness they might put two and two together. Jonas' eye problems aren't a total secret, although only a very few people know how bad they are.'

I took a drink and thought about it. Babysit a professor of ophthalmology for a few days. How hard could it be? 'These unsympathetic people,' I said, 'what would they be likely to do to Harkness?'

'There's a hell of a lot of money and influence involved. They'd be prepared to damage his hands, maybe even kill him. But if everything goes right nothing at all will happen.'

'Who's paying?'

'Funds are available.'

'Come on, Ian. There's paperwork to do.'

'Do it afterwards—wouldn't be the first time.'

That's the trouble with being flexible, people know you'll flex. I told Sangster I'd take the job. 'The professor, what hospital does he work at?'

'Prince of Wales.'

'And he has a big house where?'

'Clovelly.'

'So, he goes between them in his BMW. It doesn't sound so hard.'

'Harkness works hard and plays hard. He's a billiards nut, a golfer, and he likes to drink whisky. He also goes in for bushwalking and climbing mountains. You might find it a bit hard to keep up with him, Cliff.'

I grunted. My whisky drinking isn't what it used to be, but I play snooker and I've climbed the odd rock. Maybe I could teach the professor to surf. I said so.

Sangster grinned. 'Your first problem is getting Harkness to agree. He doesn't want to hear about having a bodyguard.'

'Who're you?'

The man moving towards me was short, about 175 centimetres; he was squarely built with wide shoulders and a thatch of thick grey hair. He wore a white doctor's coat over jeans and an open-necked shirt; his teeth gripped a curved pipe and his voice was like a pop riveter, working hard.

'I'm Cliff Hardy, professor. I'm . . .'

'Oh, yeah. The private detective. I thought I told Ian Sangster and those other fuckin' old women I didn't need a bodyguard.'

The Ophthalmology Department was in a big old stone building in the grounds of the hospital. It was nothing flash, just a small lecture theatre and a collection of offices where work seemed to go on. We were standing outside the department secretary's room. The adjoining door to

19

Harkness' office was open and I could see crammed bookcases, piles of papers, several coffee
mugs and a set of golf clubs.

'Things have changed.' Lowering my voice, I
added, 'It looks like word has got out that the
man's in Sydney.'

'Shit. You'd better come in.'

The secretary, a slim, good-looking, dark-haired
young woman, was on the phone. Harkness
winked at her and we went into his room. He
pulled off his coat and dropped it on a filing
cabinet, waved me into a chair, sat behind his
desk and began excavating his pipe. 'Ever been
to Bougainville?'

I shook my head.

'Cunt of a place, a lot of it. Some beautiful bits.
Good people—tough and smart. Jonas is a good
guy. None of this Catholic or traditionalist bullshit.
He wants the place to go ahead, but he reckons
turning the Buka Strait into a sewer isn't the way
to do it.'

'That sounds right,' I said.

He tapped ashes out of the pipe into a metal
wastepaper bin, packed it from a tin of Erinmore
flake and lit it with a match. Puffing, he said,
'They've got a lot of eye problems up there—
cataract, bit of follicular trachoma and diet-related
things. A couple of good regular clinics with
operating teams could clear it up pretty quickly
but those pricks in Moresby don't give a stuff.
Jonas' mob does.'

20

'That makes him important,' I said. 'So it's important that you operate on him without interference. Where's it going to happen? Not here, at the hospital?'

'Shit, no. This place is run by medical bureaucrats who never put a finger up a bum in anger. We're going to do it in a little private joint in Bondi. What's your background—not an ex-copper, are you?'

'No. Army for a bit, insurance investigator, then into this. You've got something against the police?'

'Plenty. Used to see them use Redfern as a training ground for the heavy squads. And I got the piss beaten out of me a few times on demos and that. I suppose some of them're all right. What did you do in the fuckin' army?'

'Fought in Malaya. Have you got something against the army, too?'

The smoke was coming out in short, quick puffs. 'Mostly a waste of time and money. The medical corps paint wounds on people and practise washing them off. Bullshit. But the army did some bloody tremendous work for us on the Aboriginal eye health project. Set up these field hospitals in the bush. Great stuff.'

'I read about that. And I knew one of the blokes you used in liaison work, Jacko Moody.'

'Great guy. Did you ever see him fight?'

I nodded. 'He could've gone a long way. Still, maybe it's good he didn't. He's got all his marbles.'

'I fixed his retinas. He came close to the white cane. What're you looking at?'

I was gazing over his head at a picture on the wall. It showed Harkness in bathers, looking chunky but firm-fleshed, on a beach with a blonde woman and two snowy-haired children.

Harkness screwed around to look at the picture. He put down his pipe and massaged the bridge of his nose where there was a red indentation. Suddenly, he looked his age, which was fifty-six, and tired. 'I sent them down to Victoria for a while.'

'Good,' I said. 'That was smart. Why not be smart about yourself, too? What's that mark on your nose?'

He stopped the rubbing. 'It's where you strap on the magnifying apparatus for operating. You're observant, Cliff. D'you play billiards?'

'Snooker.'

'Better than nothing. Drink whisky?'

'Yes,' I said.

Over the next few days I drank a little whisky with Frank Harkness and played some snooker with him—on the table in the basement of his house—but what he mostly did was work. The man was a tiger for it—early morning ward rounds, lectures, clinics, consulting, operations, administration. He was at it from 6.00 a.m. to nine o'clock at night and how he had the energy to lift a glass or a cue was beyond me. But he did, and when he went up to bed I noticed that he took sheaves of papers and journals with him. He was brusque and abrasive at times, extraordinarily patient and kind at others. I quickly found out that the thing to do was to stand up to him. Toe to toe, he'd listen to a contrary argument and sometimes take notice. Otherwise, he went completely his own way. I judged that he was a man who'd made mistakes, but not very often.

I almost made one myself on the third night. I was sleeping in one of the spare rooms in the house and, before going to bed, I checked all the doors and windows. I was in bed, reading the paperback of Rian Malan's *My Traitor's Heart*, which I'd found on Harkness' shelves, when something began to niggle at me. My .38 was on a chair near the bed; I was sleeping in a light tracksuit and had a pair of slip-on sneakers at the ready. The front gate was locked; the cars were locked; the doors were locked, but something was wrong. I put the book down, pulled on my shoes and went out into the passage. Light was showing under Harkness' door and I could smell his pipe. That jogged my memory. We'd been playing snooker in the basement and the fug from the pipe had got to me. I'd opened a small window onto a light shaft and had forgotten to close it. Just a small aperture, but enough. I padded down to the basement and closed the window. Harkness was standing at the top of the stairs when I

23

returned. He wore a striped, knee-length night-shirt. His calf muscles bulged.

'What?' he rasped.

'Nothing.'

He nodded and went back into his room but I could tell that he was edgy. So was I.

The call came the next day. My job was to get Harkness, in the mid-afternoon, to an address in Bondi without anyone knowing where he was going to be or following us. Harder to do than it sounds—Harkness' day was mapped out in half-hour grids, but we managed it. I had to hope that the people looking after Buckawa were doing the same.

The place was a small cluster of two-storey, cream-brick buildings set behind a high fence. It looked like a garden furniture factory, with all the chrome and plastic chairs scattered around, but in fact it was the William O. White Private Hospital.

'Supposed to be closed for renovation,' Harkness said as we mounted the front steps. 'But it's got a good working theatre.'

'How many people to do the op?'

Harkness took a last suck on his pipe and knocked the ashes out into a flower pot. 'Just you and me.'

He laughed at my reaction and we went through the front door into a tiled lobby where Ian Sangster was waiting with three black men and one black woman. Ian did the introductions but the only name that stuck with me was that of the biggest of the bunch, a 190 centimetre heavyweight named John Kelo, who seemed somehow to be in charge. Sangster looked worried, I thought. Harkness was in his element, shaking hands, turning on the rough charm for the woman who was evidently a nurse.

We trooped up a staircase, Harkness in front with the nurse, then Sangster and me, then Kelo and his pals.

'What's wrong?' I hissed in Sangster's ear.

He shook his head and didn't reply.

Along a corridor, Harkness talking animatedly, snatches of pidgin, laughter. One of the Bougain-villeans moved swiftly past, opened a door and stood aside. The room was brightly lit; there was a small desk, several pieces of overhead equipment that could be swung into place and a chair something like the kind dentists use. A man got up from the chair and extended his hand to Harkness, ignoring everybody else. He was built along the same lines as the doctor, but bullet-headed, bald and his skin was the colour of tar.

'Good evening, professor,' Jonas Buckawa said.

'Gidday, Jonas. Go easy with the grip, son, I'm going to need those fingers to fix your peepers. Sit down and let's take a look at you.' He gave Buckawa a gentle shove towards the chair.

One of the attendants stepped forward and grabbed Harkness' upper arm. 'Be more respectful of the leader,' he said.

Harkness shook the hand off and looked

25

furiously at Buckawa who was sitting in an upright, regal posture in the chair. 'What the fuck's this, Jonas?'

The same man spoke again. 'Do not use foul language.'

I was turning towards Sangster for an explanation when I was gripped in an expert choke-hold. John Kelo opened my jacket and slipped the .38 out of its shoulder harness.

'Examine your patient, please, doctor,' Kelo said. 'You will be performing the operation tonight.'

Harkness laughed. 'You're off your head. And I won't touch him until I hear what you bastards are on about. Jonas?'

The man whose task it seemed to be to handle Harkness raised his fist. Buckawa froze him with a look. 'Don't be foolish, Leo. You must not damage the doctor.'

Leo backed off. 'Yes, sir.'

Kelo hadn't taken his eyes off me. He nodded and the choke-hold was released. I rubbed my neck and thought about turning round to do some nose-breaking. I could feel Sangster twitching beside me. The nurse opened a door and I could see through into an operating theatre—harsh lighting, gleaming chrome, an antiseptic smell.

Harkness folded his arms. 'Forget it. I'm not operating tonight and maybe not at all unless I get an explanation for all this crap.'

'Things have changed, professor,' Buckawa said

smoothly. 'I have had visitations . . . visions . . . dreams. I am called to do great things, but my enemies are all around and I cannot stay here long.'

Buckawa's body appeared to be relaxed but there was tension in his voice and something unnatural about his unwavering stare. I remembered Harkness saying that he approved of Buckawa because he wasn't corrupt and he wasn't religious. I could only guess at what he was feeling now. He moved forward, taking a device from his pocket, and shone it into each of the seated man's eyes in turn. He snapped his fingers at the nurse and she handed him another gizmo with a headband attached to it. He slipped it on and fiddled with a control before leaning down and looking into Backawa's eyes again through the lens.

He straightened up and sniffed, felt for his pipe.

'No,' Leo said.

'Get stuffed.' Harkness took the pipe and tobacco tin out and began to go through his ritual. 'No slicing tonight, children. Pressures'd have to be monitored for three days, minimum. Have to do measurements for the intra-ocular lenses. We need an anaesthetist . . .'

'Much of that data is on hand,' Buckawa said. 'We have anticipated you. The implants and lenses are available. Sister Pali and Nurse Kwaisulia are highly competent theatre personnel. Dr Sangster can act as anaesthetist.'

27

Ian Sangster said, 'No.'

Harkness said, 'Fuck you.'

I swung hard at Nurse Kwaisulia and got him on the right cheekbone. I felt my knuckle crumple and it didn't seem to bother him much at all. Harkness dropped his pipe and tin, went into a crouch and bullocked Kelo back against the wall, driving back a man who outweighed him by twenty kilos by sheer force of will and anger. I went for Kwaisulia again but Leo stepped in and the two men grabbed my arms and held me easily. Harkness got in one good shot at Kelo's ribs but then the bigger man's strength told—he pushed the doctor away and grabbed both his fists. Harkness' hands were swallowed by those big black fingers and Kelo forced his arms down to his sides. I realised what he was doing—protecting Harkness' hands and limbs from damage.

Harkness glared at Buckawa, who had sat impassively in his chair throughout the action. 'You can't make me operate on you. That's not the way it works.'

'Things are going to work differently,' Buckawa said, 'I have already told you that. I have discovered something interesting about the concept of a free press.'

'What the fuck are you talking about?'

'Press statements have been prepared in which you announce your support for the Buka oilfield project, and your belief that the income generated will do great things for eye health in Melanesia.'

'Who'll believe that crap?'

Buckawa smiled. 'Some plants do not have to grow to full size, it is enough that they take root.'

'You're mad. What's happened to you, Jonas?'

I stared at Buckawa and noticed for the first time the Rolex, the heavy gold ring, the silk shirt and the suit. 'I can tell you what's happened, Frank,' I said. 'He's switched sides.'

Harkness bent to retrieve his smoking gear. He tucked it away in his pocket and shrugged his shoulders. 'OK,' he said. 'Let's get on with it. The sooner the stink of you's out of my nose the happier I'll be.'

Kwaisulia rumbled angrily but the others seemed unconcerned. Buckawa said, 'I hope you don't have any ideas of . . . disabling me.'

Harkness grinned at him. Thirty years of pipe smoking had worn down the tops of two of his teeth, giving him a tough, don't-mess-with-me look. 'You'll just have to take your chances, won't you, sunshine? Now which eye is the bad one? I hope I can remember to get that right.'

Kelo gestured to Leo and Kwaisulia to let me go. He took a pistol from his pocket and pointed it at me. 'You and I, Mr Hardy, though professionals, can be of no use here.'

Sister Pali opened the door and Kelo gestured for me to go out. Harkness was looking grim. He gave me a sharp nod. The only satisfactory thing I could see in the room was the swelling on Kwaisulia's face. Kelo shepherded me down the passage and into an office. I sat in one of the easy chairs and he wheeled the chair out from behind the desk and took that. Smart man; it looked uncomfortable, which is what you want to be when you're guarding a man who doesn't like you.

'Your boss is nuts,' I said.

Kelo shrugged his massive shoulders. 'Possibly. Who cares?'

'You're in it for what you can get?'

He nodded. 'There is a lot to get.'

'Why the rush? And the heavy stuff? Harkness would have done the job under the original terms. What difference does a few days make?'

Kelo didn't answer and I was left to make my own conclusions. Somehow, a few days *did* matter. Why? We sat in silence while an hour crawled past. I could have done with a drink, but Kelo didn't look like the flask-carrying, hospitable type. A tap came on the door and Leo put his head in. He and Kelo exchanged nods. Leo took the pistol and the upright chair and Kelo left the room. Leo was young and nervous. He handled the pistol awkwardly. I slumped down in my chair, wondering if I could reach his knee with a long kick, or if I could get to the heavy glass ashtray on the desk before he shot me. Doubtful on both counts.

It was the right line of thinking though because I was ready when the shots boomed outside and the glass shattered. Surprise stalled Leo for an instant but set me off: I was out of the chair, hammering down on the hand that held the gun and jabbing for his eyes before he knew what was happening. I hit his right eye and he screamed. I wrenched the gun away and clouted him with it above the ear. He groaned. Blood was leaking from his eye. I hauled him out of the chair and laid him on his back. 'Listen, Leo. You're going to lose that eye unless you lie here perfectly still. I'll get the doctor for you. But don't move. Understand?'

'Yes,' he whispered. 'The doctor.'

I checked the pistol—a .45 Colt Trooper, nice gun. Nothing was happening in the corridor but I could hear noises coming up from the lower level. There were two more shots from different weapons and shouts in a language I couldn't understand. Then silence. I eased forward to look down the stairs. John Kelo was backing up towards me with his hands in the air. Below him were two men. One stood on the bottom stair facing towards the door, the other was a few steps below Kelo; his gun was pointed up at the Bougain-villean's broad chest.

I tried to keep my voice loud and steady. 'Stand where you are. I've got clear shots at all three of you.' I proved the point by putting a round into the wall a metre from the gunman's head.

Everybody froze. The man at the bottom of the stairs also had a gun and he lifted it a fraction.

'You at the bottom. Put it on the floor.'

The man on the stairs was trying to locate me but I had a partition to hide behind and the acoustics in the stairwell were puzzling him. 'You, too,' I said. 'The gun on the step behind you.'

'Who are you?'

'When the guns are down we'll talk. Mr Kelo, plant your fat arse on the stairs.'

Kelo slowly lowered himself, keeping his hands in the air.

'We're the Federal Police,' the gunman said. 'Put down your weapon.'

I laughed and cut the sound off when I heard a note of hysteria in it. 'I hope you are, mate. But until I'm sure you'd better do as I say.'

He bent smoothly and put his gun on the stair. His right hand went into his jacket and he took out a small folder which he flipped open. 'Phillip Allen, Detective Sergeant. Can we stop this?'

Kelo came out of his crouch like a tiger. He swept up the gun, straightened, turned. I shot him in the right shoulder; he yelled, the gun flew from his hand and he bounced off the wall before falling, slowly, awkwardly, to the bottom of the stairs.

After that, it was a matter of cautious approaches and you show me yours and I'll show you mine. We convinced each other that we were PEA Hardy and policemen Allen and Blake. Kelo was bleeding badly and in shock. Blake was phoning for help when Frank Harkness came storming down the stairs.

'What the fuck's going on here? Who the fuck are you?' He confronted Allen and for a minute I thought he was going to plant one on him.

'Policemen, Frank,' I said. 'It's a bit of mess. Could you take a look at the bloke on the ground there?'

I pointed and Harkness' belligerence fell away. He hurried down the stairs and bent over Kelo.

'Ambulance is on its way,' Blake said. 'How is he?'

'Strong man. Plenty of meat on him. If they get here tonight he should be OK.'

'How's Buckawa?'

Blake was assembling weapons—he had my .38, which they must have taken from Kelo, the Colt Trooper which I'd handed over and Allen's pistol. Allen moved closer to Harkness who was packing his pipe. 'Are you Professor Frank Harkness?' he said.

Harkness nodded.

'Do you have any knowledge of the whereabouts of Jonas Buckawa?'

Another nod. Harkness, standing immediately under a No Smoking sign, lit a match.

'I'm here to interview him.'

The doctor puffed smoke and laughed at the same time. 'You won't be interviewing him for a while yet, sonny Jim. He's up there sedated and bandaged to buggery.'

Allen seemed unable to cope with Harkness' style and manner and I wondered if it was something he'd assumed long ago as a means of putting people off-guard and getting his own way. Sirens sounded outside and the ambulance team raced in followed by a couple of uniformed cops. There was a lot of talking and note scribbling. The paramedics loaded Kelo onto a stretcher and headed for the door. Then I remembered Leo.

'Hang on,' I yelled. 'There's another one. Frank, up here.'

He bounded up the stairs beside me and if there'd been another flight I think he might've got to the top first. I dashed along the passage and opened the door to the room where I'd left Leo. He was lying rigid on the floor, not moving a muscle, with his eyes closed. The trickle of blood had dried on his dark face. Harkness bent over him and the touch of his hands seemed to soothe Leo instantly.

'Open up, son.'

The eyelid flickered, then lifted slowly. I didn't want to look. I remembered how soft and jelly-like the eye had felt when I hit it. 'Frank, is it . . .?'

'Fucking mess. We'll have to get him into the theatre. Where's that other pair? They're not bad.'

Kelo was taken off in the ambulance. I rounded up Pali and Kwaisulia who were sitting quietly in another room on either side of the recumbent Buckawa. We got Leo into the theatre and I finally had time to talk to Allen and Blake, with Ian

Sangster sitting in. They told me that there were a number of new charges pending against Buckawa in PNG—fraud, embezzlement, assault—and that the Buka Strait Committee had very recently disowned him. That was news to Ian. The Committee was persisting with the lawsuits and the surveillance and Buckawa's splinter group was looking to make a deal.

'That fits,' I said. I told him about Buckawa's behaviour and what Kelo had said. 'What now? You've got a fair bit on him—illegal entry to Australia, firearms offences . . .'

Blake and Allen exchanged looks. 'Just between you and me, Hardy,' Allen said, 'I think our government wants to cooperate with Mr Buckawa, not prosecute him.'

'Shit,' I said. 'Kelo . . .'

Allen smiled. 'Got the wrong end of the stick. Like the people who gave us the tip.'

Harkness came into the room, puffing smoke and drying his hands. 'He'll be all right, wasn't as bad as it looked. You're a fucking gloomy threesome. What's next?'

'Frank,' I said. 'You and me are going off somewhere to drink a little whisky.'

Ghost Writer

The magazine was old and faded, the paper yellowed and crisp. I treated it gently, opening it to the page which had been marked by a Post-it. The article was entitled 'Death Duo' and it went for atmosphere right from the jump. I read:

A body lay on the steps. One hand rested just above the level of the water and a narrow watchband was visible above the cuff of a light-coloured coat. Dark hair curled damply to the nape of the neck. The legs were a little apart: the new sole of a woven brown leather shoe faced upwards.

No marks could be seen on the head or hands, but beside the face lay two items, a train ticket from Adelaide and a small silver rose. A dawn walker had called the police from The Rocks station; they arrived as the mist was lifting from the Opera House . . .

I skimmed another few paragraphs and put the magazine down. 'I remember it,' I said. 'Vaguely—she really made a name for herself with that piece.'

The woman sitting in the client chair in my Darlinghurst office nodded. Dark red hair waltzed around a pale, perfect face—huge green eyes, sculpted nose, cheekbones, put-it-here lips. Physically, Madeline Ozal had everything women dream of having and men lust after. Furthermore, she had a quality that was probably worth around a million a year to her as an actress—she riveted your attention so that it didn't matter what she said or how she said it, you just wanted to hear more, and watch.

'Valerie Drewe,' she said. 'God, what a bitch.'

I watched the way her lip curled. You read about it, lip-curling, actually seeing it was unnerving. 'She was a very successful writer,' I said. 'Went on from journalism into—'

Madeline Ozal's hand-waving dismissal was like a signal to take your own life without a moment's regret. 'I don't want to hear about it. I know all about her prizes and husbands and real estate holdings. She was a slut and the world's a better place without her.'

'I'm confused. I'm not used to dealing with celebrities, alive or dead. What—?'

She reached out and grabbed the twenty-year-old magazine. Its yellowed pages fluttered as she shook it. 'Valerie Drewe implied that the woman they found in the water a few hours later had killed the man and then drowned herself. That's all bullshit. All that silver rose crap—'

Vague was the right word for my recollection

of the case. It had happened before I got into the private inquiries business and I'd read about it in the tabloids and magazines like any other voyeur. 'Forgive me, Miss Ozal, but this is all old history. I'll be blunt—what's it to you?'

The big eyes filled with tears. 'Cliff, they were my Mummy and Daddy. She didn't kill him and she didn't kill herself. I was just a baby. They couldn't have.'

The whole story came out then over coffee and tissues. Madeline Ozal had been brought up by her mother's sister who was married to a Turk. Hence the name. The name on her birth certificate was Macquarie, daughter of Ernest, whose occupation was given as 'playwright', and Josephine, nee Peters.

'Madeline Macquarie,' she said. 'Not as good, is it?'

I shrugged as I made notes. 'Is it important?'

'You bet. No-one would ever have heard of Norma Jean Baker.'

'What about Meryl Streep?'

She laughed. 'You've got a point. Kurt Butler told me you weren't dumb, not that Kurt's all that well-equipped to judge.'

Butler was an actor I'd bodyguarded some years ago. I hadn't seen his name in lights lately, but it's always nice to be well-thought of, even by a has-been. Madeline Ozal was no has-been—she was big and getting bigger. 'I had a bit part in one of his movies,' I said. 'I threw someone off

39

a building or fell off myself. I can't remember which.'

She laughed again. 'In Kurt's movies it hardly matters. Look, the only people who know about my parents are my aunt and uncle and now you. But soon the whole world's going to know.'

This sounded like the nitty-gritty, worth getting a contract form out of the desk for. 'You're expecting to be blackmailed?'

'No. I'm writing my biography . . . well, I'm sort of writing it.'

Astonishment made me rude. 'You can't be a day over twenty-five. What's there to write about?'

She smiled, showing perfect white teeth, nicely spaced. 'I was brought up by an insane woman who ate twenty-four hours a day and was terrified of going to sleep on account of nightmares. Plus I've been in the movie business here and in the States for ten years. You'd be surprised. No, I'm going to reveal the truth about being an orphan in the book. It's a big selling point.'

I started to reassess her. So far, the only grounds she'd given for casting doubt on the standard account of the Macquaries' deaths was that they had had *her*. Now it was a selling point.

She leaned forward across the desk. She was wearing a white silk shirt buttoned to the neck. Nothing so crude as cleavage, but the way she moved made me want to close my eyes and count to ten. Her voice was soft and came from deep in her throat. 'It'd be a much bigger story,' she said, 'if I could prove who really killed them.'.

I put my pen down and leaned back in my chair, stomach in, chin up. 'I suppose it would.'

'That's why I'm here. Peter says it'll make a great chapter. Oops . . .' She dug into her leather shoulder bag and pulled out a notebook that had a gold pen clipped to it. 'I'm supposed to be taking notes. How tall are you?'

'Six foot and half an inch. Who's—?'

'What's that in centimetres?'

'I don't know. I was that tall before centimetres got here. Who's Peter?'

'Peter Drewe. He's helping me with the book. Are you married?'

'No.' I wrote the name on my pad and added 'ghost writer'. 'Any relation?'

'He's Valerie's son. We're lovers . . . sort of.'

'Uh huh.'

The green eyes were dry now and piercing. 'I can read upside down. Ghost writer is unkind. You don't like me.'

'I don't see how I can help you, Miss Ozal.'

She put her gold pen and suede-bound notebook away. 'Peter has some leads. We want you to check them out. We'll pay your standard fees.'

It all sounded odd, but I was intrigued by the cast of characters and the few routine jobs I had on hand would allow me to spend some time on it. I told her the damage, she signed the contract and I agreed to telephone Peter Drewe. She smiled and we shook hands. I tried not to watch the way she put on her coat, shouldered her bag, flicked back her hair. I tried.

Peter Drewe lived in a flat on the corner of Crown and Burton Streets, Darlinghurst. The building was called 'Royal Court', which was a bit too much monarchism in one address for my taste. Nice place though, good security door, wide staircase, vaguely art deco trappings. Drewe was a dark, thin, nervous type who licked his lips a lot. His one-bedroom flat was neat and admirably organised for writing and fucking. His word processor sat on a desk with fold-out attachments to carry books and papers. His writing chair was an engineering miracle. I caught a glimpse of the bedroom—mirrors, satin sheets, uh huh.

'Maddy's aunt won't talk to me,' Drewe said, after we'd kicked it around for a while. 'She doesn't approve of me. But I'm sure she knows a lot more than she's ever told Maddy.'

'Did she talk to your mother?'

'No. She wasn't in the picture then. Maddy was in hospital with some childhood illness when her parents died. The aunt claimed her about a week later. Valerie wrote her piece within forty-eight hours of the finding of the bodies. That was her way in those days, apparently. She called it "tasting the cum".'

'Miss Ozal said you had some leads. Is that it—talk to the aunt?'

'No. You could see the cop who worked on the case. One Ron Fisher. He got booted off the force later and won't talk to reporters.'

He gave me the names, addresses and numbers. 'Have you got a theory, Mr Drewe?'

He shook his head and licked his thin lips. 'Not really. Valerie said Ernest had a mistress in Adelaide and that Josephine killed him on that account. The silver rose was a gift for the mistress or from her, I forget which. My only theory is that she was completely wrong about those things.'

'Why d'you say that?'

'Why not? She was wrong about everything else in her fucking life.'

I stood in the street outside my office building. Ron Fisher lived in Gymea. My car was parked close by, about the same distance away as the telephone. You're not that keen, I thought. I went upstairs, hauled out the cask of red, drew off a glass and let my fingers do the driving.

'Fisher.' A harsh Rothmans and Toohey's Old voice.

'My name's Hardy, Mr Fisher. I'm a PEA. Frank Parker'll give you the word on me if you want it.'

'I've heard of you. What is it?'

'I wanted to talk about a case of yours. Old

one—the body on the Opera House steps and the floater.'

'Talk, then.'

'The inquests said heart failure and drowning.'

'That's right.'

'What do you say?'

'Mate, I had so many problems back then I was relieved when I came up with sweet fuck-all. They were both nuts—drunks and coke freaks. My guess is his ticker gave out on him when he was high and she thought she could walk on the water.'

'What happened to the train ticket and the rose?'

'The what? Oh, shit, who knows? They went to whoever got the effects. There'd be a record at the station, maybe. I was a D at The Rocks.'

I could hear the regret in his voice along with the bitterness. I thanked him and hung up. One thing leads to another—there's nothing wrong with visiting police stations, some of the best people do it. I drove to the station. The sergeant behind the desk looked old enough to have been in the force in Ron Fisher's time and I took the risk of mentioning his name. Coppers are clannish and whatever it was that had led to Fisher's expulsion hadn't tarnished his name among his fellows. The sergeant clicked his tongue, muttered 'Poor bugger' and obligingly sent a constable to fetch a record book dating back to the time in question.

When it arrived the book was both dusty and damp but it yielded the information: the personal effects of Ernest and Josephine Macquarie had eventually been handed over to the drowned woman's sister, Mrs Isabel Ozal. At that time her address had been in Kingsford, now it was in Dover Heights. I thanked the sergeant and handed the book back.

'How's old Ron?' he said.

'Sounded bitter.'

'Poor bugger.'

As an ex-surfer and still keen swimmer, I always see Dover Heights as a frustrating place for every-one except suicides and those maniacs who jump off cliffs with ropes tied to their feet. There's no other quick way to reach the water. I parked under some plane trees and gave the Ozal house the once-over. Nice place—end of the street, elevated double-fronted brick bungalow, 180-degree views to New Zealand and a piece of the cliff almost in the backyard.

I'd telephoned, intending to spin some yarn or other, but there had been no answer. The house looked occupied; there was a brown Celica in the driveway and the venetian blinds to the front rooms were open. Time again for Hardy to play it by ear, hoping not to get thrown out on it.

I stepped over the low gate and walked up a cement path to the front porch. The door was open and music was pouring out from the house. Italian opera, a warbling soprano and a fruity tenor.

No point in knocking, nothing could be heard over the din. I walked down the wide passage past a polished table carrying a crystal vase full of dead flowers. The dry petals were scattered across the thick beige carpet. There were two sets of rooms off the passage which made a turn to the right into a big sitting room filled with late afternoon light. Its huge windows looked straight out to sea.

A trick of the light saved me. As I faced the window I caught a glimpse of a reflection, a blur of movement above the level of my head. I jumped sideways, spinning around as the axe blade whooshed down, missing me and hitting a low glass-topped coffee table. The glass shattered, shards flew and the axe skittered away to smash into a big earthenware pot. The pot disintegrated. I struggled to get my balance amid the flying glass and bits of pottery. The man rushed at me, his fists knotted and flailing. He was small but wiry and imbued with hysterical strength. He landed a wild swing to the ribs which hurt. I ducked away from the next swing and gave him a short right to the ear. He bellowed and came at me with his hands stretching for a strangler's grip. I grabbed his thumbs, exerted pressure and he was out of action. He sank to his knees. He was in his socks and his feet had been cut by the glass. Blood flowed across the dusty surface of the polished boards.

All the fight had left him. I eased him onto

a couch. He sat there, staring at the darkening ocean view. I found the bathroom, wet a towel and came back to find he hadn't moved a muscle. I peeled off his socks and got to work on his feet. The cuts weren't deep but blood still seeped from them. I wrapped the towel around them and looked around for some anti-shock medication. There was a drinks tray in the corner of the room— I poured out two big brandies and put his in his hand. He drank it in a gulp and held out the glass for more. I obliged. The drink put some colour into his drained, haggard face. He was about sixty, olive-complexioned, with sparse iron grey hair. He wore a silk shirt that smelled of alcohol and sweat and vomit; his well-cut slacks were creased and stained. The socks hadn't been too clean, either.

'Are you Kemal Ozal?' I said.

He nodded and sipped his drink. 'Yes. She has left me. I was crazy. I thought you were the man. I am sorry.'

'Your wife has left you?'

'Yes.'

'When?'

He sat stiffly, not seeming to find it odd to be answering questions from a total stranger whom he'd tried to kill. 'They came, Madeline and the son of that terrible woman. They talked. After they went, Isabel told me that she was leaving me. She said she was in love with another man. I could say nothing, think nothing. I loved her.

47

I did not care that she became so fat. I loved her fat. She left and I began to drink. I am a Muslim. I am not used to drinking. I was sick. I took many sleeping pills but they did not work. I thought you were the man. I am sorry.'

'Is there someone who can look after you, Mr Ozal?'

The tension and rigidity seemed to flow out of him. His eyes fluttered closed, opened and shut down again. 'I am all right,' he slurred. 'Just tired.' He knocked back the rest of his brandy without opening his eyes again and slipped sideways on the couch. He snored softly. I stuffed a cushion under his head and lifted his feet, still wrapped in the towel, up level with his head. The bleeding had stopped and his pulse was strong. There may be nothing in the law books to support it, but I reckoned I'd earned the right to search the house.

Houses can tell you a lot about the people who occupy them, but only when the people actually live there and do their own cleaning. The Ozal house was very little lived in and was evidently cleaned professionally. I found nothing of interest until I got to Mrs Ozal's bedroom. It looked as if it had been searched by a mad gorilla. Clothes and shoes and spare bed-linen were scattered everywhere; a few books lay open on the floor; the contents of a writing desk had been riffled and distributed across the bed which had been moved from its usual position. Conclusion: someone had been searching for something in great haste, not the best way to do it.

I took my time, examined the furniture and fittings carefully, and, down behind the dressing table, trapped just above the skirting board, I found a small, hinged case not much bigger than a powder compact. It was elaborately carved with gold inlay and possibly made of ivory. I snapped it open. It was lined with velvet and designed to hold a small object in the shape of a rose. I turned my attention to the debris on the bed and found four pieces of crisp, faded paper—a train ticket with booked sleeper, Adelaide to Sydney, torn savagely across twice. A collection of newspaper clippings of articles by Valerie Drewe had been ripped to shreds. Several other newspaper cuttings had been crumpled. I smoothed them and discovered that they recorded radio programs for Wednesday, twenty years back. The 8.00 p.m. 'Radio Theatre' timeslot was underlined. There were also some torn photographs—old ones showing a slim, pretty woman and later pictures of the same person twenty years older and fifty kilos heavier. Kemal Ozal was sleeping peacefully when I left the house. I'd put a carafe of water with a glass and a strip of Panadol tablets on the floor beside the couch. Also a packet of Band-aids.

When I got home I made a toasted sandwich, poured a glass of cask white and sat down with a ballpoint and paper to try to figure out what

I had. The one glass became two and then three and four before I reached any conclusions. Four-glass conclusions don't always mean very much, but I called a few people I knew in the journalism business and picked their brains about Peter Drewe. As a four-glass conclusion, this one was shaping up pretty well.

After making two phone calls, one to Madeline Ozal's agent and another to Peter Drewe, I spent the morning in the Mitchell Library and then walked to Darlinghurst. I buzzed Peter Drewe's flat and he answered immediately. He met me at his door and suggested that we go up on the roof. It was a mild day, two o'clock in the afternoon, and he had a six-pack of Coopers in his hands. I agreed. We sat on upturned terracotta garden pots and looked out over the city skyline. Drewe ripped the tops off two bottles and handed one to me.

'Cheers.' He drank and wiped his mouth. I realised that it wasn't his first drink of the day by a long shot.

I sipped the beer. 'It was your idea, the biography of Maddy, wasn't it?'

'Who told you that?'

'Her agent. You made the approach. You've got a reputation as a political journalist. This is a bit out of your usual territory, wouldn't you say?'

He shrugged loosely. 'Saw the chance to make a buck.'

'I don't think so. Your mother died three months ago. A week later you made contact with Madeline Ozal. Your colleagues report on a personality change—from being a hot-shot political reporter, rooting everything in sight, you became detached, almost ascetic.'

'Bullshit.' He lifted his bottle. 'Is this being ascetic?'

'You're under pressure, son. Why don't you screw Maddy?'

'Who says I don't?'

'She implied it.'

'OK. So what?'

I produced the ivory case and opened it. 'I found it in Maddy's aunt's room. She's missing, but she tore the place apart looking for this.'

He drained his stubby and opened another. 'Go on.'

'You and Maddy went to see Isabel Ozal. Whatever you said to her caused her to leave her husband. She said she was in love with another man.'

He smiled. 'She must have weighed close to a hundred kilos.'

'Yes. I think she was lying. About now, not about then. I think she had an affair with Ernest Macquarie, her brother-in-law.'

'Proof?'

'I have some, of a kind.'

'Tell me. That's what you were hired for.'

I shook my head. 'First, you tell me what you

51

found when your mother died.' He was opening and closing the catch of the ivory case. The clicking seemed to have a mesmeric effect on him. 'One of these,' he said. 'Identical to this. Except that the rose was inside. That was typical of Valerie. Isabel might lose her rose, but not Val.'

'So, you discovered a connection between Macquarie and your mother. Who's your father, Peter?'

His smile was bleak. 'She told me she didn't know. She told me that when I was too young to understand. Later, when I was old enough to understand and saw the way she lived, I believed her.'

'Kemal Ozal knew your mother. He called her "that terrible woman". Isabel had made a collection of her articles which she destroyed when she left. What did you say to her?'

He drained his second stubby and reached for a third. His hands were shaking and he had trouble pulling the tab. I took the bottle, opened it, and handed it to him. 'Nothing, really,' he said. 'When Maddy was out of the room I told her that I knew everything. I mentioned the silver rose. I was bluffing. She didn't react at all. That's when . . .'

'That's when you decided that you might need to apply a little extra pressure. Me.'

He nodded and took a long pull on the bottle.

'Let me get this straight,' I said. 'You've spent three months taping Maddy's reminiscences of the dopey films she's worked on and the idiot

actors she's fucked because you wanted to find
out—'

'Whether we had the same father and who killed
him. Right.'

'But you didn't learn anything.'

'Not much. Her mother was a very good-looking
woman, like Isabel must have been. That seems
to have been their stock in trade. I've got a theory
that they were both part-time whores, but no proof.
Ernest Macquarie was a failure. He called himself
a playwright but he never had a play produced.
I checked with the Theatre Guild. He wrote advertising copy when he wasn't drinking, probably
when he was, too.'

'You shouldn't be so hard on him,' I said. 'I
think he was your dad.'

He glared at me drunkenly and pushed back
the lank, dark hair that had fallen into his face.
'I was afraid of it,' he muttered.

'Because you're in love with Maddy?'

'Right. Fuck it. What's your evidence?'

'It's not evidence. You don't even have to listen.'

'I have to know.'

I told him then about the collection of radio
play scripts I'd seen in the Mitchell Library. They'd
been published by a small, now defunct press
under the name 'E. Mack,' but the library had
identified Macquarie as the author. *The Silver
Roses* was about a man who had a wife and two
mistresses, one of them his wife's sister. The wife
knew nothing. The mistresses knew about the

53

wife but not about each other. Separately, each threatened to kill him if he slept with anyone other than her and his wife. The Lothario in the play liked games. He gave each of the women a silver rose and the play revolved around the danger to him when one of these roses got lost or found, I forget which, compromisingly for him.

Drewe listened in silence. When I finished he said, 'It sounds stupid.'

I stood up. 'I'm no critic, but I thought it was one of the dumbest things I've ever read.'

'You think Isabel found out about Valerie and killed him along with the wife?'

'Possibly. Or each one found out about the other and they did it together. Valerie's article could have been written to protect them by putting the blame on the wife. We'll never know.'

'What about the ticket from Adelaide? What's the significance of that?'

I shrugged. 'What does it matter?'

Two days later they fished Mrs Ozal out of the harbour. I used my contacts to get a look at the autopsy report. Her stomach was full of booze and pills and salt water. In the language of the report, they found a small silver rose in one of her 'body cavities'.

Airwaves

Wilbur Hartwell was a star announcer on a top-rating radio station until his heart attack a few years back. He took his golden handshake and went fishing the way so many men do. He was back in Sydney looking for a job within a year.

'It drove me crazy,' he told me over an illicit (for him) beer one night in the Toxteth. 'Catching fish. What's the point?'

'You should have eaten them,' I said. 'Nothing better for the heart.'

'I *did* eat them. I ate the bloody things till I couldn't stand the sight of them. By the way, how's your cholesterol, Cliff?'

'Low,' I said. 'Likewise my fat to body weight ratio, blood pressure and resting pulse rate. I had a checkup a couple of months ago.'

Wilbur, plump and rosy-faced, sighed. 'How do you do it?'

'Nothing to do with me. My ancestors did it. The way I live, I should be a hypertense, twitching wreck—or dead.'

That exchange had taken place six months back.

Wilbur, a friend of Cyn, my ex-wife, who somehow stuck on after Cyn and I broke up, settled into a job managing Radio 2IC. Funded from a thousand different sources, espousing of a thousand causes, 2IC tapped into a deep well of talent and called itself 'the voice of the inner city'. I started listening when Wilbur took over the station. I liked the chat and the music. I was surprised when Charlie MacMillan got a regular evening spot. MacMillan was a sports commentator turned general know-all. He was a born-again Christian, a political reactionary and a racist. Trouble was, he could be funny, in a beer 'n' prawns kind of way, and he did have a knack for getting people who should have known better to argue with him on air.

The Federal Minister for Aboriginal Affairs took him on, and lost, as did Phillip Adams, though he ran him close, and Peter Garrett. MacMillan rated, drawing sponsors and listeners. Some of the audience must have been like me, hovering between antagonised and amused, but there's nothing that says your audience has to be smiling. 2IC jumped a few rating slots. I was happy for Wilbur, although I could imagine his old Whitlam-ite hackles rising when MacMillan came out with lines like, 'Malcolm and Gough're great mates now, and neither of them's had an Abo to dinner since they were in the Lodge.'

Wilbur rang me on a hot November night. I'd got home after a hard day's summons serving, cracked a beer, turned on the news and put my feet up. The phone rang and I was positioned so I barely had to move a muscle to answer it. It was Wilbur.

'Not listening to MacMillan?' he said.

I hit the mute button on the remote control. 'No, I've got the TV on. Different lies from different sources.'

'Cynic. You *have* heard him though?'

'Sure. He's a prince.'

'He's a prick. But he's a money-making prick.'

'For now,' I said. 'He's a nine-day wonder. People'll get tired of him.'

'Someone's so tired of him already they're threatening to kill him.'

'That's par for the course, surely. Nuts threaten the newsreaders, the actors in the commercials . . .'

'Right. MacMillan's hate mail started after his first broadcast. He laughed about it. But this one's got him worried. He wants protection.'

'No,' I said.

'Top dollar, Cliff. Expenses paid within reason. Charlie goes to some nice places. You could meet a girl or two. He takes a break in a fortnight. That's all it'd be.'

'I hate him,' I said. 'I'd end up helping the threatener.'

'Flat rate,' Wilbur said. 'Five thousand, plus expenses.'

'You bought me. Starting when?'

'In about fifty-five minutes, when he goes off air. Pick him up at the studio. I'll have a cheque ready for you.'

'Don't push it, Wilbur,' I said, 'or I'll do my best to convert him to Buddhism.'

I'd expected a thorough briefing from Wilbur, but he'd left early for his regular poker night, so all I had to do was collect the announcer himself and a thousand-dollar cheque at the studio in Pyrmont. Charlie MacMillan had a big, mellow voice but it came out of a scrawny, undersized head and body. He dressed in thousand-dollar suits and held himself very erect, but he was still a runt. We had our first disagreement straight off.

'I'm not riding in that,' MacMillan said, eyeing my utterly reliable, if slightly elderly, Falcon.

He pointed to a white Merc sitting at the kerb. I could see the red alarm light blinking inside. MacMillan tossed me the electronic gadget that turns the alarm off. I tossed it back and he fumbled the catch. 'Don't be dumb,' I said. 'If there's anyone out to get you, why make it easy?'

He looked ready to argue, then he shrugged. 'There is someone out to get me, make no mistake about that. Maybe you're right. Drop the keys inside. Someone'll run the Merc home. I've got places to go.'

I wanted to tell him to run his own errands,

but five grand is five grand, and if Charlie took a set against me I wouldn't get it. I gave the alarm-stopper, the keys and the message to the door-keeper and we piled into the Falcon. He directed me to a block of flats in Arthur Street, Surry Hills. Security door, no parking. Good place to keep a woman on the fairly cheap. I escorted him to the door. A female voice answered when he buzzed. MacMillan winked at me.

'How long?' I said.

The door clicked and he pushed it open. 'Depends. Say an hour.'

My office was only a couple of blocks away. I could have gone there and checked on the mail. Or I could have slipped across to the Brighton and chewed the fat with a couple of the cops who were sure to be there. Instead, I bought a can of light beer and a packet of peanuts and sat in my car watching the lights in the second-floor window. A few people came out of the flats, a few went in. Others entered the restaurant across the road. A quiet night. The loudest noise I could hear was myself, crunching the nuts. A woman came out of the restaurant and, just for a second, I thought it was Cyn. It wasn't, too young. Mind games. Cyn wouldn't have been a bit surprised to find me drinking beer and eating peanuts in my car while looking up at a bedroom window.

Fifty minutes and MacMillan came out, not exactly zipping his fly, but almost. He smelled

of whisky and baby oil, not a pleasant combination. I started the motor. 'Home is where?'

'Nowhere,' he said. 'Wherever I finish up. Let's
go to the Skin Cellar. Have a good time.'

The Skin Cellar was a dive on Darlinghurst Road
which featured toxic air, watered drinks, fat
strippers and third-rate crims. MacMillan tried to
big note himself through the door, but he had
to cough up ten bucks for himself and ten for
me, just like everybody else. We were there for
three hours during which time he had ten drinks,
chatted up several less-than-keen women and got
the brush-off from a couple of minor hoods. The
only guy who talked to him was a stringer from
one of the tabloids, a fact Charlie was apparently
too drunk to realise.

I got him out into the relatively fresh air and
the cool night, absence of noise and the darkness
seemed to hit him like a brick. He sagged against
the car. I asked him again where home was
and he just shook his head and mumbled. I'd
started out by disliking him and had moved on
through despising to contempt. But what could
I do? I bundled him into the car and took him
to my place. He unzipped himself and pissed
all over the pot-plants on the front porch, which
was better than doing it in the hallway. I eventually
got him to take two aspirins with a glass of
water. In the spare bedroom, stripped, with a
wet towel beside him on the pillow, he was
one of the drunkest, most pathetic specimens

to have inhabited the spot. And that's saying something.

MacMillan was one of those people who don't suffer from hangovers. He was up at seven, cooking scrambled eggs, banging pots and pans and whistling in the kitchen. He turned on the radio— commercial station pap. I like the news and 2BL. I slouched into the kitchen and changed the station.

'Hey!' He spooned egg expertly out onto a plate.

'Hey, yourself,' I said. 'Any coffee?'

'I drink tea in the morning.'

'You would.' I made coffee and watched him eat—four eggs, three slices of toast, lots of butter and two sugars each in his three cups of tea. And he wouldn't have weighed sixty kilos, wringing wet. He seemed brimful of confidence, nothing like the burning-out wreck of the night before.

'What're you staring at?' he said.

'You. Why so chipper?'

He wiped up egg with a bit of toast. 'Got confidence in you, Cliffy,' he said, chewing. 'You're all right.'

'Call me Cliffy again and I'll cut your vocal chords.'

Tough guy stuff. He loved it. I despised myself. But it kept him buoyant through the morning and afternoon while he did the things radio personalities do—checked his phone messages, read the material his researcher had prepared for him, met with a couple of his sponsors. I had to admit it, he put in a full day, and he did it on cups of tea, mineral water and a couple of salad sandwiches. He seemed to get a bit nervous after the sun went down, scrutinised the street and traffic, hunkered down in the car. But he was in the studio again by 8.30 with a thermos of coffee and some yoghurt. No wonder he was ready to howl by eleven.

I sat in Wilbur's office and shared a bottle of red with him. Wilbur listened to MacMillan's opening spiel, which was something about who was really calling the shots in South Africa, before cutting off the feed.

'I met fish I liked more,' Wilbur said. 'What d'you make of him?'

I told Wilbur about our night and day. 'He seems to be two different people, day and night, sober and drunk. He's genuinely frightened though. When did the death threats start?'

'Day one,' Wilbur said. 'Show you.' He opened a filing cabinet and took out two folders, one thick, the other thin. He passed the thin file across. 'This is just the written stuff. We get a few over the phone and on the board when he does the talk-back segment. Use the delay switch, but there's a few tapes you could listen to if you like.'

I nodded and poured some more red. The eight or ten letters were written on a variety of stationery, some typed, some handwritten in pencil, ball-point, ink, Texta colour. They basically denied MacMillan the right to hold the opinions he espoused. A couple argued against racial differences on scientific grounds. Two letters threatened MacMillan's life if he continued to broadcast, although they were vague about how the execution would be carried out.

'What's in the other folder?' I asked.

'Messages of support.' Wilbur dumped the heavier folder in front of me. Unlike most of the brickbats, the bouquets were all signed and carried addresses. A few were typewritten or done in the copperplate they taught in state and private schools before the war; others were rougher. Their message was consistent—Australia for the Australians and that meant people with skins more or less the colour of the paper they were writing on.

Wilbur slipped a cassette into a machine on his desk and hit the PLAY button. I listened for a couple of minutes to harsh male voices, threatening violence.

'How did the message that flipped him out come?'

Wilbur shook his head. 'Don't know. He just came storming in, swearing his life was in danger and demanding protection.'

I looked through the hate mail again and listened to the tape. Then I checked the pro-Charlie stuff, including a couple of callers that had been on air and agreed with MacMillan that white was right.

'Did any of the knockers get air time?'

'Sure. A radical libber gave him a bit of a run for his money. Some bishop got on, but Charlie made mincemeat of him.'

I closed the folders and put them back on Wilbur's desk. 'There's something funny about this,' I said. 'But I can't put my finger on it.'

'Don't worry. No-one wants you to solve anything. Just keep him safe, semi-sober and happy for a couple of weeks.'

'He only drinks at night,' I said. 'During the day he's like Mahatma Gandhi.'

Wilbur had drunk most of the red and his face was almost the colour of the bottle. He belched. 'Wish I could say the same.'

'How come you're doing all this? Why isn't Charlie hiring me?'

'In his contract,' Wilbur said. 'Standard these days. Celebrities get protection, employers pay.'

'I'm all for it,' I said. 'Seeing as how it's mostly bullshit. Money for jam.'

Wilbur concentrated on pouring the last of the wine into his paper cup. 'Right. So why are you frowning?'

'I don't know,' I said. 'A feeling.'

'Feelings are for women,' Wilbur said, and he laughed.

I didn't laugh and I frowned deeper and even swore a little when Wilbur told me that MacMillan insisted on using his Mercedes to get around in. He claimed other cars hurt his back.

MacMillan did his session and we set off into the warm Sydney night. The evening was a repeat of the previous one, with variations. Charlie visited a Woollahra whorehouse and a succession of pubs around the eastern suburbs. He got thoroughly pissed and announced loudly in the last pub that he was going back to a motel in the Cross and that anyone was welcome to come along. There were no takers. We'd left the car at the lower end of Victoria Street. I had to support MacMillan, stop him bumping into trees and posts. This distracted me so that I didn't hear the footsteps until it was almost too late.

'Hey, man.'

Pseudo-matey, jumpy, vicious. I shoved Charlie away and hit the first man as hard as I could with a fist and a knee and a foot. He screeched, sagged away. His mate was coming at Charlie. I rushed him and drove him hard into the iron railing fence. He was fat and it didn't hurt him much. He swung at me—a chain, hissing in the air. I ducked under it, grabbed the metal links and brought them up, wrapped them around his fat neck. He felt the chain bite into his flab and he started to beg.

'Please, mister. I never . . .'

The other one was vomiting into the gutter. I'd got him very low with the knee. I forced the fat man to kneel beside him and I bumped their heads together, not gently.

'Stay there for five minutes,' I said. 'Make it ten to be on the safe side.'

I hauled Charlie to his feet, threw the chain away and walked him to the car. The rush of adrenalin was fading; I felt drained and a bit dirty. Automatically, I drove to the motel MacMillan had mentioned, a down-at-heel joint with a car park as skimpy as the balconies on its rooms. I wedged the Merc into the only space available, which left its MAC 1 numberplate exposed to the street.

Charlie used his Mastercard although he was almost too drunk to sign his name. We got a big room you might have called a suite if it had been cleaner—two double beds and a single, small kitchen and breakfast nook. Charlie sprawled on one of the doubles, clawed off the top layer of clothes. He mumbled something that might have been 'Thanks', and went to sleep. I made instant coffee and sat on the single bed feeling like the year's prize idiot. I knew this motel only too well— it was a crim hangout where more than a couple of the fraternity had had their last drink, fuck, heroin hit, whatever, before kissing their dirty lives goodbye.

I spent a very uncomfortable night drinking coffee, watching old movies on TV and nodding off in a chair I'd selected particularly for its lack of comfort.

MacMillan woke up at seven, clear-headed, as before. I'd ordered breakfast at six, just for something to do. He wolfed down most of it, cold eggs, tomato slices and the kind of limp toast only motels can provide. He flicked through the paper and whistled as he slapped more butter on the toast.

'Quiet night, Cliff? Easy money?'

I grunted. Light glinted around the edges of the heavy blind. I reached over and released it. The bright sunlight hit him full in the face. He barely blinked.

'Ah, Sydney,' he said. 'You beauty. What would you say to a swim?'

The man was a freak. I was beaten. 'Wouldn't mind.'

'That's the spirit. I've got nothing on today. You like Newport?'

I liked Newport. Who doesn't? I'd have liked it even better if I'd had the kind of place Charlie had to live in—a white painted sandstone house on a hill overlooking the ocean; high wall all around, nice garden, balconies, roof deck, plus one of the best burglar alarms and security systems I'd ever seen.

Charlie made a few calls from one of the several phones in the house. He found some swimmers for himself and an old pair of stubbies for me. We went to the beach with towels, chilled mineral water and about ten pieces of fruit. MacMillan turned out to be a real little wave-cracker. He swam out strongly, using the slight rip to get him beyond the breakers and he came in, head down, shoulders hunched, streamlined.

I caught one to his three, quit about ten waves sooner, and went to the bottle shop for a few cans of Coopers Lite.

It's hard to feel angry when you're lying in the sun, munching crisp apples and wetting your whistle, but I managed it. I knew MacMillan was playing me and Wilbur Hartwell for suckers. He was exposing himself, as it were, instead of keeping a low profile and staying safe inside his electronic fortress. The trouble was, his fear was genuine. As we lay on the beach, he twitched every time a male over sixteen walked past. His shades came on and off as he gazed around at the car park, the surf club, the skateboarders on the pavement ten metres away. A truly frightened man. But what of?

I crumpled the second can and stuffed it into the plastic shopping bag we'd used to carry the towels and stuff. Charlie eyed the two remaining cans but he shook his head when I offered one. 'Never touch it in the daytime.'

'Wilbur showed me your hate mail,' I said.

He popped a warm can of Taurina Spa. 'Yeah?'

'But that's not what got you scared. Tell me about it.'

'Nothing to tell. Phone call. Black bastard, threatening to off me.'

'How d'you know he was black?'

He grinned and did a good imitation of the slightly guttural, slightly harsh tone that characterises the speech of a lot of Aborigines. 'You can tell a Koori talking, can't you, Cliffy?' He jumped up, spraying sand on me. 'C'mon, got to get back to work.'

We went back to the house. I had a quick shower in one bathroom, he had a long one in another. That gave me time to prowl in his study and find things I wasn't surprised to find.

I was getting used to driving the Merc, liking it, even. Maybe Charlie'd give me a job as his permanent minder and I could drive Mercs and body surf and drink at night until my brains turned to mush. In my mind's eye I could see Cyn nodding her head. *Go for it, Cliff. Sleaze is what you love. Admit it.* I wouldn't admit it. As I drove Charlie MacMillan to his late afternoon appointments, I worked on a headstone inscription, while he used the car phone to get the day's news, gossip and headlines from his researcher. The best I could come up with was: 'He left the world no dirtier than he found it.'

We got back to the studio about half an hour before Charlie was due on air. A quick skim of his researcher's material and he was ready. I drifted into Wilbur's office, ransacked his drawers and played with paper and plastic tape while Charlie MacMillan told a story about his uncle who'd fought in World War II:

'Uncle Ted said, "The Germans were clean fighters, but the Japs were animals." I'm quoting a man who fought for this country from 1939 to 1945. That man's views are worthy of respect. Think about that!'

'You think about it,' I said to the speaker on the wall. 'You lying bastard.'

I was ready to tackle him when he finished his stint, but he gave me no time. He barrelled out through the sound studio door, pulling on his jacket and fumbling for the car keys. 'Come on, Hardy. We're not paying you to sit on your arse. Let's roll!'

I followed him out onto the street to tell him what he could do with himself, and that's when they arrived. Two of them, and not junked-up punks this time. Pros. One had a sawn-off and the other a baseball bat. MacMillan stopped dead when he saw them, retreated a step and looked around for me. The guy with the shotgun pointed it at Charlie's head. It was pure reflex on my part— I cannoned into Charlie, knocking him down. I had my .38 in my hand before he hit the ground and I fired at the gunman, going for his legs but hitting him higher. I lost my balance, fell on my elbow and dropped the pistol. The street light caught the varnish on the bat as it whipped through the air and shattered Charlie's shoulder. He screamed. The bat went back in an arc; the hitter was taking his time, aiming, and the return swing would've reduced MacMillan's right knee to fragments. I scrabbled on the cement for the shotgun, grabbed, raised and triggered it, left-handed. The charge hit a pair of legs in blue jeans, ripping the fabric, shredding the flesh. Another scream. The bat fell free and the man followed it down, hard.

After that, there were cops and ambulances and pressmen. Temporarily, as the relatively uninjured party, I was almost the villain of the piece. Mac-Millan said I was a hero. That was just before they sedated him. It made me feel dirty. I gave a statement to the police at the Glebe station and Wilbur arrived to back me up. The reporters had followed Charlie and his assailants to hospital. I felt like something washed up on the beach.

A constable bought coffee in plastic cups from an all-night place in Glebe. Good coffee. He also offered cigarettes. I refused. Wilbur accepted. The constable lit him up.

'What gives?' I said.

'The Ds will tell you, Mr Hardy.'

Mister, I thought, *must've done some something right.* I had. A detective sergeant explained that identifications had come through. The two men I'd shot were well-known enforcers, gambling debt collectors and frighteners—contented sadists with long records.

'Brent Burke's going to have a plastic stomach and Tommy Mather'll be on sticks. For life, with luck,' the cop said. 'Thanks.'

Wilbur drove me back to where I'd parked the

Falcon in a side street near the 2IC studio. On the way I told him how MacMillan had faked the hate calls—verbal and written—and conned his employer into providing him with protection.

'Jesus,' Wilbur said. 'Gambling?'

'Yeah. He's got books on gambling systems— cards and horses. He's got three typewriters and he practises writing left-handed. Does a pretty good Charlie Perkins imitation, too. He might do it on air one day, if you're lucky.'

'You're pissed off,' Wilbur said. 'I'm sorry.'

I patted his shoulder which hurt my jarred elbow. 'Not at you, mate. Not at you.'

Charlie MacMillan was back on air, with his shoulder in plaster, more popular and racist than ever, within a fortnight. He sent me a note explaining that by having me around he was just buying time until he settled his gambling debts. He hadn't been expecting anything heavy. He claimed to have been so broke that he couldn't afford to hire anyone good. Anyone like me. But he was in the clear now and he enclosed a bonus cheque for five hundred dollars. I signed the cheque over to the Aboriginal Legal Aid Service in Redfern and mailed it to them. Maybe they banked it, maybe they burned it. I don't know.

A month after he returned to the airwaves, MacMillan was gambling in a Dixon Street club.

He went to the toilet and a man, described by witnesses as 'of Asian appearance', followed him. MacMillan was found ten minutes later, lying on the tiled floor, with his large and small intestines overflowing the blocked toilet bowl.

Cadigal Country

Henry Hathaway lowered his well-padded buttocks onto my unpadded clients' chair and said, 'How long have you lived in Sydney, Mr Hardy?'

'All my life,' I said, 'bar a few periods overseas.'

'And how long have you . . . practised as a private enquiry agent, if I may ask?'

'Sometimes that seems like all my life, too, but I guess it'd be about twenty years.'

'You must have seen some changes in that time?'

That didn't seem worth a reply. I grunted and waited for him to get to the point.

'When I first came here in the mid-'50s, Australia was still essentially British. Anglo-Celt, as they say. You know what I mean?'

His accent was English with an Australian overlay. I'm mostly Irish myself, with some English and French thrown in. Or so my sister, who's interested in such things, once told me. I said, 'What can I do for you, Mr Hathaway?'

Maybe my tone was rougher than I'd intended, or perhaps he liked to meander on. Anyway, he took some offence, got red in the face and glanced

at the door. I didn't like him but I couldn't afford
to lose him. He looked prosperous. I gave him
one of my I'm-the-soul-of-discretion-and-reliabil-
ity looks and watched him smooth his own
feathers. He patted his abundant silver hair and
stroked his fleshy chin. He liked himself enough
for the two of us.

'I have a daughter, Fiona. She's nineteen. I
discovered that she has been keeping company
with an entirely unsuitable person.'

I wrote 'Fiona Hathaway, 19' on my notepad.
'What's his name, this person.'

He sniffed and got the words out with difficulty.
'Alberto de Sousa. I imagine you know the foreign
enclaves of Sydney pretty well, Mr Hardy?'

I put my pen down and shrugged. 'Not really.
Vietnamese in Cabramatta, Lebanese in Newtown,
Italians in Leichhardt.'

'Portuguese?'

'You got me.'

'In Marrickville, specifically Petersham. A section of New Canterbury Road has nothing but
Portuguese shops—butchers, real estate agents,
fruiterers, videos. Everything!'

I had a vague idea of where he meant and an
impression that he was exaggerating. I looked at
him across my scarred desk and said nothing. A
lot was going to depend on what he said next.

Mr Hathaway leaned forward and lines of concern furrowed his face. 'I'm a widower, Mr Hardy,
and Fiona is my only child. I love her very much.

I don't want her ruining her life over a worthless criminal.'

That hooked me. The man had problems. I told him my rates and he barely listened. I opened a file on him. He was fifty-nine years old, a retired electrical engineer with investments. 'I have a heart disorder,' he said. 'Irregular rhythms. It's an electrical problem, the doctors tell me.'

I thought he might smile at the irony of that but he didn't. Mr Hathaway was heavy going. He went on to tell me that his daughter had met Alberto de Sousa when he had delivered a load of party liquor to the legal firm where Fiona worked as a secretary.

'His family has a bottle shop in Petersham. A restaurant too, I believe.'

'Both good earners,' I said. 'In the right locations and properly run.'

He ignored me. 'They aren't even Europeans.'

Back onto that. It was hard not to be testy. 'Portugal's in Europe. Last I heard.'

'The de Sousas are from Madeira. D'you know where that is?'

'I'd be guessing,' I said. 'Off the coast of Spain?'

'Off the coast of *Africa*!' he hissed. 'They're no better than niggers.'

He took his chequebook out of his pocket as he spoke. I thought of the rent on this office, the mortgage in Glebe, the Bankcard. 'You said something about Mr de Sousa being a criminal.'

You don't become a private investigator to

inflate your ego or get a rosy view of human nature. Hathaway told me that he'd hired Richard Maxwell two weeks before to do the job he was now offering me. The reason? Maxwell was English. I knew him. In the Private Enquiry Agent fraternity he was known as 'that poofter Pommy pisspot'. Prejudice, it's everywhere.

'Mr Maxwell became ill,' Hathaway said. 'He's hospitalised, in fact, and he had to give up the case. But he did tell me that Alberto de Sousa has a criminal record and that he is involved in criminal activities.'

'What else did he tell you?'

Mr Hathaway had a knack of saying the right thing just often enough. 'Nothing relevant,' he said. 'He's a very sick man, I gather. But he did recommend you.'

Hathaway wanted me to accumulate evidence on Alberto de Sousa's criminality which he could either present to the police or put before his daughter, depending on the seriousness. A psychologist would probably have told him his plan wouldn't work. Nothing stimulates the young as much as persecution by the old. But I was a detective, not a psychologist. I had the skills for the job and I needed the work.

I got a few more details, deposited Hathaway's cheque and set out to find Richard Maxwell. He had a flat in Surrey Street, Darlinghurst, but he operated mostly out of a pub on the corner of Liverpool and Palmer Streets. This put him just a few doors from a gay brothel and a church. Maxwell was known to frequent both. At the pub I got the information I expected: Dick was in a Potts Point detox clinic. It was early December, too hot and sticky for walking but that was still better than driving through the heavy traffic, breathing carbon monoxide and pushing up the blood pressure. I crossed William Street, made my way through Woolloomooloo and walked beside the water to the McElhone steps which I went up very slowly, keeping in the shade. As I climbed, I tried to recall everything I knew about Portugal. I ran out long before I reached the top—sweet wine, Prince Henry the Navigator, Vasco da Gama—that was about it.

The clinic was in a three-storey brick building which had once been a block of flats. Two streets back from Woolloomooloo Bay, the clinic's upper floor would afford a view of the water on two sides—maybe that was where you got to when you'd been clean for a month. If so, Dick Maxwell had a way to go. I found him watching TV in a ground-floor room. Despite the warmth of the day, he was wearing pyjamas, a dressing gown and slippers, and he looked about seventy, although he was only a few years older than me.

'Stay away from the gin, dear boy,' he said after I'd sat down next to him and used the remote control to mute the TV. There were two other

79

men in the room but they didn't object to the loss of sound. They were gazing at the moving images, smoking and trying to think of reasons for staying alive without alcohol.

'Is that right, Dick?' I said. 'I'm safe then. A gin-and-tonic once in a while. That's my limit.'

Maxwell nodded seriously. 'Harmless, that. I drink it like water. Brush my teeth with it. That's why I'm here in this far-from-stimulating company.'

He was a ruin—all broken veins, sagging skin and bloated features. He was alcoholic, homosexual and English. I wondered how Henry Hathaway had reacted to the combination. I brought the name up and stated my business.

'Ah, yes,' Maxwell said. 'A professional referral.'

I gave him a twenty-dollar note and showed him that I had several others to hand.

He pocketed it. 'Shoot,' he said, 'metaphorically.'

'You told Hathaway this de Sousa had a criminal record. Expand on that.'

'Juvenile stuff,' Maxwell said. 'Graffiti, joy-riding —fines, bonds, a community work-order.'

I gave him another twenty. 'You also said he was still involved in criminal activity.'

Maxwell nodded. 'I watched the young chap for a few days. Rather a pleasure, if you follow me. He's up to something—clandestine meetings with other young blades, phone calls from public boxes, you know the form, Clifford.'

Twenty again. 'Any idea what it's all about?'

Maxwell shrugged. 'No. I'm afraid I started to turn Hathaway's retainer into clear liquid rather early in the piece. He might steal the whole of his father's stock—and that's a great deal of booze, let me tell you. Or they could be planning to knock over the Petersham RSL club one fine Saturday night. That'd be a nice score.'

'Did you put in any work on the daughter?'

Maxwell rolled his eyes. 'Scarcely. An insipid-looking little blonde piece. Possibly quite tough underneath. But not a patch on Alberto.'

I gave him another twenty and wished him a speedy recovery.

'Don't mock, dear boy. The only cure is sobriety and as Oscar said, that's not a cure, it's a calamity.'

I walked back to St Peter's Lane, collected my Falcon and drove to Petersham. The block-and-a-half of shops along New Canterbury Road did feature a fair number of Portuguese establishments, but not a majority. There were a few more around the corner in Regent Street, along with a Chinese laundry and a Commonwealth Bank. Interesting, but it didn't exactly amount to little Lisbon. The de Sousa liquor store was a big barn of a place with a laneway on one side and a restaurant on the other. I found a semi-legal parking place near the post office and walked back. It was late afternoon on a Friday and the grog shop was busy. The stock was impressive and there were pallet-loads of wine and spirits on special. I grabbed a couple of bottles of Jacobs

Creek riesling at a lower price than I'd seen for years.

'Alberto!'

A heavy-set, middle-aged, dark man shouted from the rear of the shop. A young man at the counter who was dealing with customers while clacking keys on a computer, looked up. A quick exchange in what I took to be Portuguese followed and the older man scowled and looked very unhappy. The younger one hit the cash register key viciously but smiled as he took my money and made change quickly. He was tall and lean, in his early twenties, and no darker than I am myself after a week or so at the beach.

Hathaway had told me that young de Sousa worked in the liquor store by day and did a stint in the restaurant at night. I wandered around for a couple of hours familiarising myself with the area. I sat for a while on a bench in Petersham Park. Nice place—well-tended oval, small grandstand, Moreton Bay figs and a swimming pool tucked into one corner. The big, hand-operated scoreboard still held the proceedings of Saturday's second-grade cricket match. The board was partly in shadow, but from where I sat I could read one of the entries: Kazantsakis 58. The Petersham RSL club was a big, garish joint with wide steps, glass doors and a look that said 'Forget your cares and spend your money'.

I had whitebait and salad and two glasses of wine in the de Sousa restaurant. The place was moderately busy with a clientele of southern Europeans, Asians and Anglos. Alberto waited table as if he didn't like doing it very much but wasn't going to screw up in any particular. Later, I sat in my car in a side street and watched the back exit of the restaurant. At 10.30 Alberto came out, got into a blue Laser and drove off. I followed him. So far, I hadn't seen anything to criticise in the kid. He worked hard. He even drove a Ford.

First stop for Alberto was the underpass west of Petersham station. A few small fluorescent tubes didn't do much to dispel the darkness. The tunnel was a gloomy, graffiti-daubed slimepit smelling of piss. Alberto conferred briefly with a man in biker gear. Small objects changed hands. Next point of call was a pub in Newtown. He ordered a light beer and sipped at it without interest. I knew the pub by reputation. I went past him and down the steps to the toilet where I took a leak. One of the two cubicles was closed with no sounds coming from within. I went back up to the bar in time to see Alberto check his watch. He went into the toilet and wasn't there long enough to unzip his fly. He walked straight through the bar, ignoring his barely touched middy.

I followed the Laser to the Cross and left Alberto in Darlinghurst Road, talking to a young blonde with four-inch heels and a three-inch skirt. I drove home to Glebe, stowed the Jacobs Creek in the fridge and went to bed.

The next day was Saturday. Alberto worked in

the shop until noon, emerged eating a sandwich and swigging a can of coke, and headed south. He turned off the Princes Highway into the national park, crossed the Audley weir, took the turnoff to Maianbar and drove to a small timber house on the edge of the settlement.

Maianbar is one of those anachronisms—a small pocket of freehold land within a national park. It consists of a few unpaved streets off the main road, maybe a hundred houses and a general store. At low tide you can walk around the beach to Bundeena and get a ferry to Cronulla. Otherwise, the only way out is by road. Cyn and I had spent a let's-try-to-patch-this-marriage-up holiday there years ago. Good holiday, no soap on the marriage. The house de Sousa went to was at the end of a rough track, surrounded by bush. I approached on foot, using the abundant cover. I saw two cars besides de Sousa's, two other men and one woman. They sat on the front veranda, talked and drank coffee. They argued, then calmed down. I'd have given a lot to be able to hear what they were saying but there was no way to get close enough. When the group showed signs of breaking up I scooted back to my car and got it out of sight down another track.

All three cars left and I walked back to the house, intending to break in. The woman sat on the veranda fiddling with something on her lap. I squinted through the bush, trying to make out what she was doing. Suddenly, she lifted a pair of heavy binoculars and started scanning the landscape. I ducked back under cover and squirmed away through the scrub to my car.

On Sunday I thought about it. On Monday I decided to have a look at Fiona Hathaway. She left her father's large terrace house in Macauley Street, Leichhardt, at 8.15 and caught a bus into the city. I rode along with her. She was pretty, blonde, nervous-looking; fashionably and expensively dressed in a pale linen suit and cream silk blouse, but without the confidence those sorts of clothes usually give a woman. She sat in the bus, staring straight ahead of her. Maxwell had thought of her as possibly tough underneath a conventional exterior. I wasn't sure. There was something unusual about her, but I couldn't identify it.

She walked from George Street to an office building in Martin Place. I watched the lift go up to the third floor, killed half an hour and went in, pretending to be lost. I got enough of a look-around to see that Lilly, Braithwaite & Reade was a big, prosperous legal firm and that Miss Fiona Hathaway was the assistant secretary to a clutch of the associates. She had her own cubicle, almost an office. I went to my place of work and handled routine matters for the rest of the day. At five o'clock I trailed Fiona home. It was hot and she carried her linen jacket, but she wore her long-sleeved blouse buttoned at the wrists.

She got off the bus two stops early and went to the Leichhardt library. I followed her in and browsed around, keeping her in sight. She lingered in the travel section. I was nearby, in geography and local history. I consulted an atlas and found that Madeira was indeed closer to Morocco than Portugal, but not by much. A history of Marrickville told me that the district had originally been inhabited by the Cadigal band—fifty or so Aborigines speaking the Dharug language. By 1790 only three Cadigals survived.

Fiona took her selection to the desk and I sneaked closer to get a look. She had three books on Portugal.

'Have you been to Portugal?' the librarian asked as she entered the books in the computer.

Fiona looked nervous and dabbed at her face which was perspiring, although the library was air-conditioned. 'I'm hoping to go soon,' she said, 'on my honeymoon.'

That'd be news to her dad.

I had a lot and I had nothing. Plenty of tracks but nothing to actually shoot at. Alberto was scoring smack, consorting with prostitutes and conducting secret meetings in the bush. Fiona thought she was going on an Iberian honeymoon. What the hell was going on here? And what was I supposed to do? I could keep up the surveillance on Alberto, take a few infra-red snaps and lay it out for Hathaway and his daughter. I could also tell Hathaway about Fiona's wedding plans. But something told me that what I was seeing wasn't the reality. Alberto the pusher, Fiona the bride—it didn't feel right.

I followed her back to Macauley Street, noting the quick, nervous way she walked, the mannerisms that suggested insecurity, or something else. My car was parked nearby and had collected a ticket. Another expense for Mr Hathaway. I drove to Petersham, intending to watch Alberto, maybe even front him. As it turned out, there was no need. I parked in a lane behind the liquor store and, as I was locking the car, I became aware of the blue Laser that had drawn up behind me to block the exit to the lane. Alberto got out of the car and wrapped his right fist around a heavy bunch of keys. I had two keys and an NRMA tag on a single ring. I also had a .38 Smith & Wesson on my right hip under my shirt-tail.

Alberto approached me, waving the loaded fist. 'I want to talk to you. Why're you following that woman?'

I moved away from the car into open space. He was as tall as me, lighter, but much younger and maybe quicker. 'What woman?' I said.

He had the fist cocked and he was well-balanced. He wore jeans, a T-shirt and Nikes. Good fighting gear. 'You were on the bus,' he said. 'You followed her to the library, then you followed her home.'

'You've been doing some following yourself,' I said.

He feinted at my head with his left and threw

the right low. Good move, like something Fenech might have taught him at the Police Boys' Club. But he hadn't done it often or seriously enough to quite bring it off. I stepped back, made the punch miss, and clipped him on the side of the jaw with a short left. He lost balance and I gave him a bit of elbow and shoulder to help him on his way down. He fell, but he bounced up quickly and tried a roundhouse swing at my head. Another feint, but this time his feet were doing the work. He kicked me on the inside of my right thigh and I felt the strength drain from the leg as I buckled. He shuffled like Ali, but couldn't decide whether to punch or kick. I dropped my head and butted him in the stomach with the last of the leverage I had. We both fell, me on top. I kneed him fairly hard in the crotch, splayed my fingers and exerted pressure on his staring eyeballs.

'Keep very still,' I gasped, 'or get badly hurt.'

He froze. 'OK, man. OK.'

I eased away slowly, plucking the keys from his hand and letting him see the gun in mine. 'I want to talk, too,' I said.

He said, 'It's not that heavy, man. I'm just trying to save one junkie.'

I put the gun away, kept the keys and let him sit up. We sat on the kerb in the lane. He lit a cigarette and told me about Fiona and her smack habit and how he wanted to help her kick it.

'I saw you score in the underpass, again in Newtown and maybe again at the Cross last night.'

He shook his head. 'I didn't score in the Cross. I talked to a couple of the girls about what it's like, trying to get straight. It's rough. I've been building up a supply. I'm going to take Fiona away . . .'

'To Maianbar?' I said.

'Yeah, right. You really have been on the job. Are you a nark?'

'No. Go on.'

'I'm going to take her to Maianbar and taper her slowly and get her clean. I've got some friends who'll help.'

'Why?' I said.

'I love her.'

'How'd she get hooked?'

He turned his head to look at me. There was a slight swelling under his jaw where I'd hit him and some bruising around his eyes, but he was ready to take me on again if he had to. 'The guy responsible is dead,' he said.

We struck a deal, Alberto and me. I agreed to obtain some clean heroin, not the street crap he'd been scoring, and to get a doctor in on the cure. He agreed to let me tell Henry Hathaway what was going on.

'I can't believe it,' Hathaway said. 'Not my daughter.'

We were in the living room of his house—polished boards, Persian rug, cedar furniture. 'It happens,' I said. 'Think about it—how jumpy she

89

is, the long-sleeved blouses. Track marks. She met the wrong man at the wrong time. Now she's met the right one.'

He shook his head. 'A bloody wog.'

I leaned closer to him. 'Let me put you straight. He's risked more for her already than you ever have. The man who introduced her to heroin isn't with us any more.'

Hathaway's high colour leached away. 'God,' he breathed.

'Yeah. And Alberto's risked being busted and fingered buying the stuff to help her with the cure. D'you think scoring heroin's fun? It isn't. And I'll tell you something else. His family doesn't want him to have anything to do with her.'

'They know? About Fiona's . . . problem?'

'Of course not. She's Australian. She's not a Catholic. They don't think she's good enough for him.'

Fiona took her annual leave and went to Maianbar with Alberto and his friends. Dr Ian Sangster, the medico who helps keep me together, supervised the tapering and the cut-off. He tells me that Fiona's chances are good because she has love from outside and self-esteem from within. I got a big cheque from Henry Hathaway and an invitation to Fiona and Alberto's wedding which was a great bash. They went to Portugal for the honeymoon. A happy ending, so far.

Kill Me Someone

'I'm at my wits' end, Mr Hardy. I know he's serious about it. He's tried twice with pills.'

Gabrielle Walker dropped her head so that I couldn't see her red-rimmed, frantic eyes. Her thin shoulders heaved and she sighed. She was too tired to weep. I went past her, out of my office and down the hall to what the agent for the building refers to as a 'kitchenette'. In fact it's a couple of square metres of dead space beside the toilet fitted out with a sink and a power point. I've tried leaving a Birko and instant coffee and long-life milk in there to give the place a homey look, but the stuff always gets stolen. I ran the water until it cleared and took a glass back to Ms Walker. From the way she looked, anything stronger would have laid her out.

She thanked me and sipped the water. 'Sorry,' she said.

I said, 'It's OK. You've obviously had a rough time and you have a big problem. I'm not sure I can help you with it though. It sounds like something for counselling.'

She'd told me almost nothing. Just that her boyfriend was trying to kill himself. I didn't even have his name. She was a thin, intense type, with a pale face and a mop of curly dark hair. The hair danced around her face now as she shook her head vigorously. 'No. We've been through all that. This is different. I heard about you from Renee Kippax.'

Renee ran a sandwich bar and coffee shop in Palmer Street. I'd had a lot of breakfasts and lunches there, eaten on the run or taken away in paper bags, over the years. When she had a problem with some characters who were trying to persuade her that she needed plate glass, coffee machine and upholstery insurance, I helped her out by persuading them that she didn't. She was a smart, tough, independent woman whose protective instincts would be brought to a high pitch by this helpless young woman. But she wouldn't mention me without good reason.

'Maybe you should tell me what you told her,' I said.

'Andrew McPherson's his name. He's a couple of years younger than me. I'm twenty-seven. He had a terrible life as a child. His father was a drunk who came back from time to time to bash him and his mother. She went mad. But Andrew battled on. He went to tech and he's got a good job.'

I was scribbling to get this down. I interrupted her to give me time to catch up. 'Tell me what you do first, Ms Walker. I gather you work around here?'

She nodded. 'At the ABC. I'm a researcher and production assistant.'

I was back on the pace by this. 'And what does Mr McPherson do?'

'He's an art designer for magazines. He works at . . .'

She stopped and looked at me. It's something you get used to in this business. You're a problem-solver and people want your help, but their first instinct is to mistrust you.

I said, 'Ms Walker, if I went around telling people's employers what I've been told in con-fidence, I'd be out of a job in a month.'

'I'm sorry. Renee said you were very trust-worthy.'

Not quite the point but what the hell. She told me that McPherson was the art director for Bigtime Publications, an outfit that published sporting and technical magazines. 'It's a smallish firm, really,' she said, 'despite the name. And it struggles some-times when people don't pay their bills. But it's surviving and Andy has a future there. Except that . . .'

She didn't have to complete the sentence. I've encountered a few suicides in my time, some successful and some near-misses. A version of the old Samuel Goldwyn line applies: if people don't want to live you can't stop them.

Desperation or the look on my face or maybe both caused her to blurt the next words out: 'He's hired a hit man to kill him!'

93

After that, we got to the guts of it. McPherson had last tried to kill himself two months ago. After he was released from hospital, he saw a counsellor, took some anti-depressants and seemed steadier. Ten days ago, Gabrielle Walker had heard him talking on the phone, using what she called 'frightening language'.

'I tackled him and he admitted what he'd done.'

'Which was?'

'He said he'd made an arrangement with this man to kill him some time within the next three years.'

I stared at her. This was a new one. 'Go on.'

'It's terrible. He's been wonderful ever since— cheerful, funny, happy. He's done some great layouts and he did a freelance thing, a book cover, that was just brilliant. I've never seen him more . . . alive.'

'What does he say?'

'He won't talk about it. He wants to make love all the time, but he won't talk. All he'll say is that he can't face the idea of living for five or ten or twenty years, but he can face three years. And the knowledge that he might only have to face a week, or less, makes him feel good.'

'He's a very disturbed man,' I said.

'I know. But I've never seen him happier. He's never been more . . . passionate. I'm sorry, this is embarrassing.'

It was, a bit. She was a rather proper young woman essentially—restrained, even conventional. As I talked to her, I sensed that she had found

McPherson's suicidal impulses understandable, almost acceptable. She was a little low on self-esteem herself. Maybe that was what had drawn them together initially. But this twist, this variation on the theme, really threw her. She would have coped better with a suicide pact, perhaps. These were very deep and murky waters for a simple boy from Maroubra. I resorted to the oldest gambit of all. 'What do you want me to do, Ms Walker?' I said.

Her head came up defiantly. 'I want you to find this man and tell him not to kill Andrew. Tell him that you know all about it and if anything happens to Andrew you'll tell the police. That should stop him.'

I nodded. 'It would, you'd reckon. But this is a big city and there are a lot of dodgy people in it. Even if Mr McPherson's not just romancing . . .'

'He's not. I'm sure.'

'OK. But you can see why I'm doubtful. Maybe the *idea* of being killed makes him feel better. It doesn't mean there's reality behind it.'

'I know the man's name,' she said.

That, of course, put a different complexion on it. She said McPherson talked in his sleep and that she'd heard him say, 'Do it, Clark. Please do it, Clark,' over and over.

'Just Clark? Not Clark somebody or somebody Clark?'

'Just Clark.'

Ms Walker seemed to think that was enough for a halfway decent detective to go on, especially

95

one who'd been recommended by Renee Kippax. I thought it was one notch above nothing at all, but, at least partly, we PEAs are in the reassurance business. I got her address and phone numbers, took a very small amount of her money and promised I'd look into it.

You could say I went through the motions. I talked to a few people—a cop, two other private eyes, a journalist and several drinkers in several places where some of the dodgy people I'd referred to hang out. The recession was biting down there too, otherwise I doubt whether I'd have got the nibble I did in the public bar of the Finger Wharf Hotel, Woolloomooloo.

'Clark,' Mick 'the Dingo' Logan said. 'Seems to me I did hear of a guy who called himself Clark sometimes. What's it about, Hardy?'

'As far as you're concerned, Dingo, it's about thirty bucks—if your information's any good.'

'Heavy stuff?'

'It could be.'

'Clark, Clark.' Logan lit a cigarette, puffed on it a few times and then limped off in the direction of the telephone. The Dingo had had some bad luck a while back and got both his legs broken. Then he served a stretch inside and the legs didn't mend too well. His armed robbery days were over but he still knew what went on and was prepared to sell a titbit or too as long as it didn't put him in any danger to do so. That was what the phone call was about. I sipped my middy of old and waited.

Logan came back, grinning and snapping his fingers. He stubbed out his cigarette and took a long pull on the beer I'd bought him. 'It all comes back to me,' he said.

I put a twenty and a ten under my glass and looked at him.

'Hey,' Logan protested, 'you're getting it wet.'

'Dingo, you'll just turn it into beer anyway. What's the difference? Let's hear it.'

It was early afternoon on a chilly, windy day. The kind of day that turns the streets of the 'Loo into cold wind tunnels. There were very few people in the bar and they were all minding their own business. Logan leaned closer to me, whispering out of long habit. 'Word is, this guy Clark's either a bit of a joke or an undercover cop.'

I lifted his glass, put the twenty under it. 'Go on.'

'Yeah, like he claims to have form in the west or South Africa or some fucking place. But no-one knows him over here. There's a whisper he did a bank in Rockdale. Cowboy job. Could've been a come-on.'

There's no body of men more paranoid than crims when they're sober or more trusting when they're drunk. Without the lubrication of alcohol, the clear-up rate of the NSW police force would only be half what it is. I put the ten on the bar between us.

'And?' I said.

'It's a joke for sure.'

'If it's funny, I'll laugh.'

He took the money. 'He'll do a hit for five grand.'

I produced another twenty. 'Tell me where to find him.'

Logan, being the man he is, gave me three addresses and two names. Never in his life had he been known to deliver up information straight. In the old days, I'd have had to make a decision—would it be better to give him more money or lean hard and persuade him to be more precise? But everyone's become more devious since those times, and more hungry lately. Besides, Logan was almost a cripple. I bought him another beer, thanked him and left the pub. I'm more devious nowadays as well—I positioned myself where I could spot the Dingo and follow him, whether he limped, drove himself or rode.

He came out of the pub and hopped into a taxi which he'd apparently called from inside. I was right behind him, up Bourke to Oxford Street and through to Paddington. Like I said, alcohol is the fuel of criminality. Logan paid off his cab outside the Five Ways Hotel and took himself, and my fifty bucks, inside. Trendy place, for the Dingo—restored to its former glory, painted in colonial colours and with as many vines growing out of pots as could be crammed into the available space. It wasn't one of the addresses he had given me. I parked a few doors from the pub and walked back, fishing sunglasses out of my pocket and getting ready to do my imitation of a private detective on the job. In fact I knew that if Logan had another couple of beers it would be possible to belly up to the same bar and not be recognised.

The poet who said something about standing and waiting should be the official laureate of this trade. I watched men and women enter and leave the Five Ways for the next fifteen minutes. About half of the males could have been hit men or cops and a certain percentage of the females could have been males. When I judged that Logan would have absorbed two schooners, I went into the public bar. Logan was drinking at the far end, near the dartboard. He looked anxiously at his watch and lifted his glass with an unsteady hand. I got behind a pot-plant that seemed to have wandered in from outside and did some more watching. A big, beefy guy in a blue suit came in and spotted the Dingo. He had sparse blonde hair cut short, and a red face with a deep cleft in the chin. I didn't know him and from the way he moved, as if he expected everyone to get out of his way, I didn't want to.

He ordered a scotch and ice and appeared to be ready to give Logan about one minute of his time. The Dingo said something quickly in his ear and cleft-chin scowled. He grabbed a handful of Logan's jacket and polo-neck sweater and hustled him straight towards the toilet door. The action was so quick and neat that I was the only person in the bar who noticed. I went after them. Steep steps dropped away immediately inside the door. I heard scuffling sounds and went down the steps fast and quiet. Cleft-chin had Logan bent forward over a hand basin. He was so big it was hard to see the Dingo's body at all, but I could tell that his feet were scrabbling for a purchase on the slippery tiles and his head was getting wet. The big man was running water with his right hand and holding Logan's head down with his left.

I came up behind him and jabbed my .38 Smith & Wesson hard into the base of his spine. His head lifted and he saw me in the wall mirror behind the basins. I ran the muzzle of the gun up a few vertebrae and then moved it away.

'Let him go,' I said, 'or I'll make you a worse cripple than he is.'

Logan spluttered, pulled free and headed for the door. The big man let him go and I could feel him ready to turn his aggression on me. I backed away and kept the gun steadied on his wide mid-section.

He shook water from his hands, some of it in my direction. 'You're not going to use that,' he growled.

'You can't be sure.'

'I'm sure.' He moved forward, getting balanced.

The door opened and a man came in with his hand already dropping towards his fly. His jaw dropped when he saw the gun. 'Hey,' he said weakly, 'what is this?'

'Stand aside,' I said. 'I'm a police officer and I'm arresting this man. You're coming with me, aren't you, Clark?'

He swore, bullocked past the man at the door and went up the stairs. Three steps up, he kicked back savagely at me. I was ready for it. I grabbed his leg and jerked him down. He bounced against the wall, flailed his arms for a split second and then fell clumsily to the bottom. He landed heavily with his ankle turned under him. The would-be toilet user was gaping.

I grinned at him. 'He slipped. You saw it, didn't you?'

The man nodded.

'He'll probably claim police brutality.' I gestured for Clark to get up. He did, testing the ankle gingerly. I prodded him with the gun. 'Up you go and mind your footing. For a big man, you're very clumsy.'

I put the gun away and we went through the bar without attracting attention. Clark limped convincingly, but I held myself ready to plant my foot in the back of his knee if he suddenly got mobile. There was no sign of Logan on the street. Everything looked normal—light traffic, pedestrians hurrying to keep warm. I was struck by the bizarre thing I was doing. Clark seemed to sense my confusion. He stopped in the middle of the pavement and jammed his fists in his pockets.

'OK, hotshot,' he said. 'What's this all about?'

'Why were you heavying the Dingo?'

Clark grinned. The cleft in his chin flattened out and made him look even meaner. 'He was giving me some bullshit about someone looking for me. He didn't want to say who. I was persuading him.'

'Me,' I said.

'Well, well. I can't say I'm pleased to meet you. In fact, if I thought my ankle'd stand up to it, I'd punch your fuckin' face in. What the fuck do you want?'

It wasn't something to talk about there on the street. I grabbed his arm, jerked him off balance and propelled him a few steps towards my car. 'C'mon. I'll give you a lift.'

He swore and hobbled. I held him up, still pushing; he couldn't get any leverage and had to go with the pressure. At the right moment, I shoved again. He lurched forward and had to grab at the car for support. I opened the door and pushed him in. He lifted his foot out of the way quickly as I slammed the door. I moved around and got into the driver's seat, ready for him to try something nasty at close quarters. He didn't. He was curious. He took out a packet of Camels and a lighter. He lit up and I wound down the window.

'So?' he said.

I told him who I was and the nature of my business. He smoked in short, jerky puffs. He nodded and grinned when I said the name Andrew McPherson. When I finished talking he took a last, deep drag and flicked the cigarette past me and out the window.

'That Logan better crawl under a rock,' he said.

'Kill him, would you?'

He laughed. 'I never killed anyone in my fuckin' life. Never would. Mug's game.'

'I'm glad to hear it. So, it's just a scam, is it?'

'Yeah. Right. Look, Hardy, I don't want you on my fuckin' back, so I'll tell you about it. I take ten per cent up front and I don't do anything. What's going to happen? Do you think Mrs Fuck-nuckle's going to go running to the cops and say "This guy didn't kill my shitface husband the way he promised"? Like hell she is.'

'Wasn't this a bit different? The hit actually hiring you himself?'

He waved one of his big hands dismissively. 'Bullshit. All bullshit. Tell him from me he's as safe as . . . what the fuck is safe these days? How about my lift?'

I leaned across him and opened the door. He laughed, eased himself out and hobbled off back towards the pub.

I phoned Gabrielle Walker and gave her a suitably edited version of what had happened. 'I don't think you have to worry,' I said. 'How's Mr McPherson?'

'Cheerful. But he still thinks he's doing something clever and solved his problem. It's terrible

103

for me. I don't know what to do. But thank you for what you've done, Mr Hardy.'

'Is he getting any help at the moment? Psychiatric help?'

'No. Nothing like that.'

'Maybe in time you'll be able to talk about this. Tell him that he's not going to be killed. It's out of my line, but I'd talk to him if you think it would do any good.'

'Perhaps. Not now. But thank you again, Mr Hardy.'

So, I left it there. What else was there to do? It was hard on the woman, but if McPherson had bought himself some kind of weird comfort for five hundred bucks, that was his business.

Two weeks later she phoned me at home, at five o'clock in the morning. 'You bastard,' she sobbed. 'You bastard. You told me it was all right. You told me . . .'

It took me a few seconds to place the voice, distorted by grief and anger. 'Ms Walker. What happened?'

'He's dead! Andrew's dead. He killed him. God damn you, you bastard!'

She hung up. I gripped the receiver and tried to take in what she'd said. I was still half-asleep. Impossible. I started phoning and eventually got onto a Detective Sergeant Belfanti who was handling the investigation of the deaths of Andrew McPherson and Reginald Clark Cook.

'Cook a big guy with a cleft chin?' I asked.

Belfanti was terse. He told me to get down to the Edgecliff police station immediately. I was there in twenty-five minutes and shown into the detectives' room. Belfanti was a young, well-groomed smoothie, learning to be tough.

'Sit down, Hardy. How did you get onto this? It only happened a few hours ago.'

'McPherson's girlfriend.'

'Tell me.'

He switched on a tape recorder and I told him. He listened impassively, scribbling notes with a gold pen. When I finished he looked up.

'Really fucked up, didn't you?'

I didn't reply.

'You've got contacts in the force. You didn't think it'd be a good idea to talk to someone about this prick? This Cook?'

'I thought I'd handled it.'

'You handled it all right. Miss Walker and McPherson had a blue. She told him how you'd handled Cook.'

'Jesus,' I said. 'Tell me what happened.'

'Simple enough. McPherson went after Cook with a gun—.22 rifle, if you want to know. The witness says McPherson got Cook out of bed and started blasting. Cook took seven bullets, but he got McPherson.'

'Who was the witness?'

'Some whore Cook had with him. McPherson winged her too. Pity you weren't around, Hardy. He could've taken a shot at you.'

Lost and Found

'It's Colin, Mr Hardy. I know it is!'

She'd shown me a photograph and told me it was of her husband. A wife generally knows what her husband looks like, but I was sceptical. The photo was clipped from a local newspaper— the *Eastern Suburbs Courier*—one of those free rags full of civic news and real estate ads, not renowned for the quality of anything—photographs, paper, accuracy. The picture was of the Petersham Lawn Tennis Club Men's A Grade team which had beaten the Coogee team in a semi-final of the club competition.

I put my finger on the rather blurred head of a man turned slightly away from the camera. 'Him?'

Mrs Andrea Cook nodded. She was an attractive, somewhat care-worn, woman in her mid-thirties. She looked as though a few hours more sleep per night and a few hundred extra bucks per week would've transformed her into someone much more vibrant. She had told me that her husband had disappeared while swimming at Apollo Bay in Victoria four years ago. She and Colin Cook had been married for four years. They had a child and Colin had conducted a successful, small-scale building and consultancy business.

'How small?'

'Col built mudbrick houses, yurts, wattle and daub, that sort of thing. You know?'

I said I didn't know and she filled me in quickly on the details of alternative house-building in Victoria in the mid-'80s. Apparently, special government-backed loans and even grants were available for people prepared to build their own houses out of local, environmentally-friendly materials. But the builders needed plans, advice, land-use approvals, and modifications to their solar, naturally-insulated, low-maintenance fantasies. That was where Colin came in. He built a mean mudbrick open-planner and he also had the technical and economic know-how and the political skills to steer projects through the grant application minefield into council-approved heaven.

'Sounds like he was on a winner,' I said.

'For a while,' Andrea Cook said. 'But bad times began in Victoria earlier than most people think. The grants and loans started to dry up. The councils started to get scared of the greenies, especially in the country. They began to worry about how *real* environmentalists would feel about the rivers and creeks being toxic sewers for half the year.'

There was a passionate, iconoclastic note in her voice and, just for an instant, I could see this

mild-mannered, suit-wearing middle-class woman as a denim-clad, headbanded greenie, chained to a fence or lying in the mud in front of a low-loader.

'So what happened?' I said.

'The business got into trouble. Colin owed money to people who wouldn't wait and the people who owed *him* money couldn't pay. He was tense, withdrawn. We fought. He drank. We borrowed a house from some friends at Apollo Bay. Col went swimming one morning and didn't come back. The water was rough that day. I still loved him. It was terrible.'

She told me that Cook had had a paid-up life insurance policy and, while the company wasn't happy with the circumstances, she got a payout. Not the full amount, but enough to settle the most pressing debts.

'They weren't as bad as Col had made them out to be,' she said. 'That puzzled me, but it stopped the insurance company from insisting on invoking the suicide clause.'

She said she came out of the legal battles with enough to finance a move back to Sydney where she'd come from.

'I'm a Maroubra girl and I went back there. You're from Maroubra too, aren't you? My solicitor—I was seeing him about something else, but I sort of steered him round to talking about private detectives—told me about you.'

Indeed I was. I'd been ocean-dipped, salt-sprayed and maybe skin-cancered there at least ten years before her. I had no intention of going back, though. The solicitor's name didn't ring a bell, but it was a bond of some sort and the job didn't sound too hard on the operational level. The emotional side of it might get a bit sticky for Andrea later if the man did turn out to be her husband and not David Richmond, the way it said in the photo caption. But that wouldn't be my problem.

She smiled when I said I'd help and, as I suspected, a smile improved her looks a lot.

'Did your husband have any brothers or cousins? This could be a family resemblance.'

'No,' she said. 'No brothers or male cousins.'

That made it time to caution her. 'This sort of thing happens, Mrs Cook. Men take off and start new lives, new families.'

'I have to know,' she said. 'If you find that it is Col and what he's doing, I'll think about what to do next.'

That seemed fair enough. She was a qualified pharmacist and had a job in a Maroubra shop that was doing OK. She was buying a flat and could write a decent cheque. I got a six-year-old photo and some details on Col: born Melbourne, 1952; 180 centimetres, brown hair, olive complexion, solid build; no spectacles, hearing aids or false teeth. I looked at the photo. Like the man in the clipping, he was wearing tennis gear. He held a racquet as if he knew how to use it. Maybe.

'Was he a good tennis player, your husband?'

'Oh, yes—very good. A schoolboy champion.'

'Any peculiarities? I mean scars or birthmarks, anything like that?'

She shook her head. 'No. Nothing. He's a very normal man. In every way.' We both noticed that she was using the present tense. She took another look at the clipping before handing it to me.

'You've talked to someone about it now,' I said. 'That can help in itself. You're still sure?'

Firm nod. 'When can you . . .?'

'Today,' I said. 'But it could take a while. I'll be in touch.'

I waited until she'd gone before lifting up the L–Z. It doesn't look impressive but it often works. Not this time though—no Richmonds in Petersham, Stanmore or Marrickville. Worth a try. I phoned the tennis club and was told that the competition players practised on Friday evening. Tomorrow. That was OK; I had bills to pay, phone calls to make, people to meet.

The Petersham Lawn Tennis Club was on Stanley Road, Marrickville. I hadn't expected to find any actual grass courts there, but I was wrong. There were three in a group behind a dozen or so with the usual synthetic surfaces. I parked in the street and took a look at the courts, feeling nostalgic. There used to be a lot of grass courts around Sydney, green in winter, bare and yellow in summer. Bastards to play on, with their uneven surfaces and tricky bounces, but in the 1950s grass was the *real* surface, like at Wimbledon, Forest Hills and Kooyong. These survivors were well-maintained and the people playing mixed doubles on two of them were having a good time.

The serious business was taking place on a hard court near the clubhouse. I wandered through the gate, behind the social players and took up a position near the court. It was after six but with daylight saving in operation, the light was good. So were the players. Two men were playing a hard-hitting singles, going all out, whipping top and underspin shots across court and rushing the net at every opportunity to make punching volleys. I watched a few games. Both had grooved, kicking serves and good footwork. The difference emerged in the third game—the shorter guy was a fraction faster and had a little more variety in his game. When he had to scramble for a shot he did something quirky with it. He won more of the points that mattered.

Two men sat on a bench outside the clubhouse watching the play. They wore tennis gear and exchanged remarks from time to time about shots made and missed. One of them was the subject of my enquiry. Height is hard to judge when the person's sitting, but 180 centimetres seemed about right. He had the pleasant, open face and the square shoulders of the Colin Cook in the photograph. There was a fair bit of grey in his hair, but then, the photo was six years old. Col was getting on for forty now. Still only maybe. I moved a bit closer. A few of the social players wandered around. They looked respectfully at the men I was watching. Tennis obviously had its serious side at the Petersham courts, although I could see the illuminated Tooheys sign near the driveway to the clubhouse and, from the sound of it, some of the activity inside was more social than sporting.

'Help you, mate?'

One of the pair watching the players had got up and fronted me. Evidently I'd ventured a bit deep into private territory. Maybe he thought I was a spy from Leichhardt or Waverley. I was caught on the hop and couldn't think of anything clever or devious to say, not that there was any real need.

I said, 'I wanted a word with David Richmond.'

He shrugged. 'After the set, all right? Dave and me have got a bet on.'

I looked across at the court. The two players had come off. The score must have been 6–1. David Richmond was standing mid-court waving a ten-dollar note.

'OK,' I said, but the man I'd been talking to was already on his way. He went onto the court, put his ten bucks along with Richmond's under a spare racquet, and took up his position. He hit a ball to Richmond who whacked it back, flat and hard. I turned my back on the court and walked away. Colin Cook had held his racquet in his right hand and had absolutely nothing unusual about him, according to his missus. Dave Richmond hit a classic, one-fisted backhand, like Rod Laver or John McEnroe—left-handed.

'He's left-handed, Mrs Cook.'

'Oh.'

I didn't know whether to say I was sorry or not. I had her clipping and photograph on the desk in front of me and I'd made out a refund cheque for some of the money she'd paid me. I told her on the phone I'd be sending these things in the mail.

'Are you sure?'

'Quite sure. It would be impossible for a right-handed person to play tennis like that. I once saw Boris Becker change hands to reach a shot, but that was just a little flick. Mr Richmond's left-handed.'

'But he does look like Colin?'

'I'd say so, yes. Older, of course.'

'Of course. Well, thank you, Mr Hardy.'

And that was that, or so I thought. The Cook file became one of the very slimmest in my drawer and I got on with other business. Two days later I was walking towards my front door when David Richmond stepped from behind the overgrown vines that fill up most of the garden. The weapon he was holding looked like a cut-down .22 rifle. He had it levelled at my belt buckle.

'I want to talk to you, Hardy.'

I felt for my keys. 'You don't need the popgun for that.'

'Keep your hands clear.'

'Keys.'

'Bugger the keys. We're going to my car. The gun'll be inside my jacket but still pointing at you. Don't get any ideas.'

From the way he spoke and moved I concluded that he was serious. That made him dangerous and obedience the best policy. He guided me towards a Volvo parked two cars away from my Falcon. He opened the front and rear passenger doors on the kerb side and told me to get in the back. I did and he flicked the door closed and was settled in the bucket seat, turned around and with the gun pointing at my chest, before my bum hit the vinyl.

'Right. Now you tell me what you were doing out at the tennis club the other night. Said you wanted to see me, but you sloped off.'

I shrugged. 'Case of mistaken identity, Dave.'

The freshly cut, raw metal end of the rifle barrel jerked a fraction. 'That's not good enough.'

'Have to do, until you tell me how you found me and why it matters so much.'

It was dark inside the car, just a little of the street light seeping through, but I could see enough to detect something odd about his face. It had an artificial look, as if it didn't quite belong to the person behind it. He said, 'One of the people playing on the other court recognised you. He's a cop, or was. Said you were a private detective.'

'When you asked around?'

'Right.'

'Why?'

The noise he made was exasperated and angry. At that range a .22 bullet can kill you. He was sweating and I could feel something potentially very harmful building up inside him. I said the first thing that came into my mind. 'Do you know someone named Colin Cook?'

He sighed. 'Shit. Is that what this's all about?'

'Is for me,' I said. 'Looks like you've got bigger problems.'

'Let me get this right. Someone spotted me, thought I was Colin, and hired you to check on me?'

'That's right.'

'Who?'

I shook my head and didn't say anything. He sat and thought while I examined what I could see of the gun. Cheap pea rifle, basically; sawn-off barrel and stock, solid magazine, maybe twelve-shot, semi-automatic. Very illegal, very nasty, but hastily contrived, not professional.

Abruptly, he said, 'The word on you is that you're more or less honest.'

'Thanks,' I said.

'Your client legitimate? I mean . . .'

'I know what you mean, Richmond. And I'm

getting a bit sick of this. Yeah, legitimate, solid citizen, parent, taxpayer. What the hell are we doing here?'

He slid the safety catch forward and pushed the spring that released the magazine. He caught it as it fell free.

'Empty,' he said. 'There's just one bullet in the breech.'

I managed a derisive snort. 'Thanks a lot. One's all it takes.'

'I'm not a killer, Hardy,' Richmond said. 'Let's talk. Have you got anything to drink in that dump of yours?'

David Richmond didn't look like a drinking man. He had a hard, disciplined, compact body and there was no spare flesh around his face. But he put his first scotch down in record time and held out his glass for another. He'd left the .22 in the car, so I poured willingly.

'I knew Col Cook,' he said. 'How much have I got to tell you before you open up?'

'More than that,' I said.

'Right. Well, I met Col in Victoria. I was designing houses and he was building them.'

'Yurts and such?'

His eyebrows shot up, animating his face somewhat. Under the light tan it still retained a tight, unnatural look. 'You know about yurts?'

'Not really. Go on.'

117

'All kinds of weird materials and designs—circular, like the yurts, cylindrical, crystal-shaped. The banks were lending money for land and building like never before. Col and me worked on a few projects together, then we both got burned when a couple of things went wrong and the funds started to dry up.'

I sipped some scotch and nodded. So far, his story jibed with Andrea's.

'Well, we were both in trouble. Then this opportunity came up. One of our clients had a big dope plantation near Castlemaine. Col had a truck. I had a secure telephone and reasons to pay lots of calls on people. Neither of us had any criminal associations. It went well for a while.'

'Then?' I said.

'It went bad. There was opposition. To cut a long story short, Col ran over a guy with the truck and killed him. It was put down as an accident but it preyed on Col's mind. He'd had some kind of Quaker upbringing. That's how he got into the alternative lifestyle thing. He went nuts.'

That didn't sound quite right. 'What about his family?' I asked.

Richmond shook his head. 'He didn't have a family. He was a very secretive, lonely type. Always going off on his own. Hard to get to know. Hard to understand.'

'He had a wife and a kid,' I said. 'She spotted a photo of you.'

'Jesus. I didn't know.'

I poured us both some more scotch. 'Go on.'

'Well, the operation folded. We'd both taken a good whack out of it. Col comes to me one day and tells me he's sent most of his money to the wife of the bloke he'd run over. Then he breaks down. I try to steady him but he rushes off. Next I hear, he's drowned off some beach. I got scared. I thought he might have left a letter for the police or a lawyer or something. He might have put us all in the shit. I didn't know about the wife and kid. I thought he'd offed himself. Was it an accident?'

'That's what the insurance company decided.' I put my hand up to my face, tapping my cheek. 'What about this?'

'Col and me looked pretty much alike as it happened. When he shot through that night he left some stuff behind, including his passport. I didn't have one. I went to this doctor in Melbourne and got a bit of plastic surgery done. Didn't take long or cost that much. I used the passport and went to Thailand.'

'Why Thailand?'

He shrugged. 'I've got friends there and plenty of Aussies pass through. You can get the news from home. Six months and no news, so I came back, settled in up here.'

I sat and thought about the story. It could have been true. On the other hand, Richmond might have killed Colin Cook and stolen his money. He looked prosperous—the Volvo was newish, his clothes were good. For a man who had done a little criminal activity six years ago his behaviour when I turned up seemed like an over-reaction.

He saw my scepticism and touched his face. 'Plastic job turned out not so good.'

'You could have it done again,' I said. 'You look to have the money.'

'What's that mean?'

'I'm wondering whether to believe your story.'

'I left the gun in the car, didn't I?'

'I'm wondering why you had it in the first place.'

He looked around the room. 'You could be taping me.'

I laughed. 'The only tapes here go from Benny Goodman to Dire Straits.'

He sighed. 'OK. OK. I made a couple of deliveries from Thailand. No problems. I've burned the passport and I'm a hundred per cent legitimate now, but . . . it leaves you edgy.'

'So it should,' I said. 'Drug couriers are arseholes in my book. So you chopped down your rabbit shooter and came to see if I was a narc or someone connected with your deliveries?'

'Yeah. I improvised.'

'You seem to be pretty good at doing that. I still don't know whether to buy your story or not.'

He put his glass carefully on the floor and stood up. 'What difference does it make? We don't have any beef, do we?'

'I suppose not. What's this legitimate business you're in now?'

'I've got a little health farm and sports centre at Bowral. I'm the tennis coach, as well as the proprietor. I keep a flat in Petersham, too. I like those grass courts. Do you play tennis?'

'Not in your league,' I said. 'OK, Richmond. I don't like you but I believe you. Why don't you grow a moustache? There's a nice woman in Sydney who doesn't need to see that face in the papers.'

We were in the hallway, moving towards the front door. He stared at me with his oddly bland eyes. 'You're a strange man, Hardy.'

'I'm in a strange business,' I said.

The Big Lie

Robert Adamo was a slender, medium-sized man with a slow, disconnected way of speaking. 'Mr Hardy, I hope you can help me,' he drawled. 'I've never hired a private detective before.'

'There's a first time for everything, Mr Adamo,' I said. 'I don't ask as many questions as an accountant or cost as much as a plumber. What's the problem?'

He glanced around my office for a moment, which is all the time it takes to register the minimal furniture and non-existent decoration. 'I want to find someone. That is, I saw her yesterday, but . . .'

'Hold on. Who're we talking about?' I'd already written Adamo's name and address on a foolscap pad, along with the fact that he ran a picture framing and art restoration business in Paddington. Then I'd written MP for missing person, and drawn the male and female symbols and a question mark.

'Valerie Hammond. She's my fiancée. We were going to be married in two months.'

I scratched out the male symbol. It took a bit of hacking and slashing through Adamo's reticence and shyness, but I eventually got something I could put down in point form on the pad. Adamo and Valerie Hammond had met when she'd come to collect a painting she'd had framed. They got engaged after six months. The date was set; then Valerie Hammond disappeared. She moved out of Adamo's house, where she'd been living for three months, quit her executive job with Air France and dropped out of sight.

'So you had an argument,' I said. 'What about?'

'No argument. Nothing. I asked her to marry me. She said yes. Then she was gone.'

'What did you do?' I said.

His long, bony hands were in his lap now, twisting and flexing. They were strong-looking hands, and Adamo himself was a strong-looking man—straight dark hair, firm chin, high cheekbones. 'I . . . I looked for her, but I didn't know what to do. She took her clothes and she got a reference from Air France. She's very good at languages.'

It was a better start than some. Adamo was a very well organised guy: he had a recent photograph of his girl, who was a blonde with a high forehead, big eyes and a sexy mouth—165 centimetres, fifty-five kilos. I did the conversions to the old system on my pad. Valerie was twenty-five to Adamo's twenty-nine; she'd learned French, German and Italian from her Swiss mother, and she and Robert had had a lot of fun in Leichhardt restaurants. His people were Italians who'd come out in the sixties when Roberto was a small boy. He was Robert now, and his Italian was rusty. I got the rest of the dope on Valerie—parents both dead, no siblings, only friends known to Adamo were Air France people he'd already talked to with no result. Valerie Hammond seemed to lead a quiet, very constrained life.

'Sorry to have to ask,' I said, 'but does she have any . . . peculiarities? I mean does she smoke a lot, or drink or gamble?' I gave a little laugh to help the medicine go down.

Adamo shook his head. 'Nothing like that. She is very quiet, a very private person. That's why I'm dealing with you rather than the police.'

'What does she spend her money on? She'd be on a good salary with the airline.'

'Don't know. We never talked about money. I'm very careful about money. Running a small business isn't easy.' His eyes flicked around the office again and I could sense him weighing up incomings and outgoings the way I did myself, periodically. 'All I can tell you is that she's careful about it, too.'

I made a note on the pad. 'She must've saved a bit then. You don't know what bank she used?'

He shook his head. 'She didn't have any money.'

'Excuse me, Mr Adamo, but you don't seem to have known a lot about the woman you were going to marry.'

'*Am* going to marry,' he said fiercely, 'when you find her.'

I nodded. His firmness deflected me from that approach. 'Tell me about seeing her yesterday.'

'In Terrey Hills. Mona Vale Road.' He checked his watch. 'At half-past three. She got in a Redline taxi and drove away. I was in my van. I'd been delivering a picture I'd restored.'

It turned out that he'd tried to follow the taxi but couldn't do it. I'd have been surprised if he could; following taxis is a lot harder than it sounds. He also didn't get the taxi's number, which was disappointing but not fatal. I took the photograph and got addresses and phone numbers and $300 from him—two days' pay—and told him I'd phone him within forty-eight hours.

'I love her,' he said. 'No matter what.'

'There could be problems you haven't anticipated, Mr Adamo,' I said. 'Emotional things . . .'

He shook his head. 'I deal with artists every day. I know about such things. They're a part of life. I want Valerie for better or for worse.'

He was serious and I was impressed. He lived in Lilyfield, only a hop, step and jump from Glebe, where I live. I could always drop in on him and take a look at the coop Valerie had flown. Unlikely to be necessary; people can be hard to find, but it's a matter of categories. Clean-living, good-looking quadrilingual blondes who get reference from their employers aren't as hard to find as some.

It's not often in a missing persons case that you have the luxury of two clear, fresh trails to follow. As I get older, luxury appeals to me more. I rang Redline Cabs and spoke to a guy I know there who helps me because I once helped him. He undertook to find out from the service dockets which driver had picked up a fare in Mona Vale Road, Terrey Hills, approximately twenty-four hours ago, and to put me in touch with him or her.

Then I rang an employment agency which had once provided me with a typist when I needed one to make up a long and largely fictitious report. Amy Post was the typist; we'd had a brief, non-title, sexual bout and had remained friends. Amy was an executive in the company now.

'Amy? It's Cliff Hardy.'

'God, so it is. Let me guess—you need a physiotherapist who can do bookkeeping and house repairs.'

'I don't need anyone. I . . .'

Amy's voice went smoky. 'We all need someone, Cliff.'

'Sometimes,' I said. 'Right now, I've got a profile of a person who's left a job and is looking for another. I'll give you the details, and you tell me where she goes looking. Okay?'

'Okay. She, eh? Hmm.'

'It's business. A man's paying me to find her.'

Amy's voice went professional. 'Shoot.'

I gave her the details, such as I had, of Valerie

127

Hammond's age, appearance, qualifications and experience. Amy said, 'Fluent in all of 'em?'

'So I understand.'

'Half her luck. She wouldn't need to be out of work a minute. And with a good reference? Shit, she could walk in anywhere and ask for top dollar. Got your pencil sharpened? No joke intended.'

Amy gave me a list of eleven likely employers—airlines, travel agents, convention organisers, consultants. I noted down the addresses and numbers and the names of her contacts at each place. Efficiency was Amy's god, and that was one of the things that had kept our affair light—she'd sensed that my ramshackle operation ran the way I liked it, and in a manner she couldn't bear. I drew a line under the last entry and thanked her.

'Glad to help. Are you sure this chick's a job of work for you?'

'Yes. Why?'

'Nothing. Just that she sounds interesting, and she'd be earning a hell of a lot of money. Bye, Cliff.'

I hung up and thought about what she'd said before dialling the first number. I'd made a dollar sign on the pad when I'd been getting information from Adamo. I underlined it and put another question mark beside it, and the word 'bank'.

The next hour was a minefield of answering machines, indifferent secretaries, hostile underlings and the occasional cooperative person. My spiel was that I was representing a legal client who needed to contact Ms Hammond, and Amy Post's name was my calling card. I positively eliminated eight of the organisations and was left with just three—Air Europe, a new charter flight operation that could get you anywhere as long as you could pay the freight; a package holiday outfit which specialised in booking clients into off-the-beaten track hotels; and a consultancy that arranged computer linkups and interpreters in certain European locations. I could expect calls from these three when Amy's contacts were available and their commitments permitted. I made a separate note of the addresses—my time is important too.

Then I felt a little stir-crazy and went out for a drink and the paper. It was a cool, early November day, and the city seemed oddly quiet. There was nothing of interest in the paper, and I had to get out of the pub fast after one drink—it was the sort of afternoon you could easily spend in a pub, hanging around until the afternoon became evening and the evening night, and all you'd get out of it would be a headache. It wasn't so far to the Redline depot in Surry Hills and I decided to walk it and tell myself I was working.

'You missed him,' Bernie, my satisfied ex-client, said. 'Name's Wesley.' He waved at the phone on his desk. 'Be home now. Call him if you like.'

I sighed and called the number he gave me. Wesley had a deep, tuneful voice and sounded very tired. He remembered the fare.

'Where did you drop her?' I asked.

'Lindfield, I think. Yeah, Lindfield.'

'At a house, block of flats, what?'

Wesley's deep yawn came down the line. 'In the street, brother, just across from the railway station.'

I swore, apologised to Wesley and got his address in case I needed to talk to him about his impressions of the woman. Another question now and I was sure I'd hear him start to snore.

'No go, Cliff?'

I put down the phone. 'Tougher than I thought it'd be.'

Bernie clucked sympathetically and went back to his work.

That's the way it goes; one minute you think you can solve the whole thing between lunch and afternoon tea, and the next it's all questions and no answers. I went back to the office and looked at the three illuminated zeroes on the answering machine. No calls. I sat down and wrote up my notes on the Hammond case so far, the way the *Commercial Agents and Private Enquiry Agents Act* of 1963 requires you to do. I also completed the notes on a couple of other cases which had either been resolved or had petered out. Full of virtue, I drove home to an evening of TV news, spaghetti, red wine and Len Deighton. I worried on Len's behalf about the effects on his fiction of the Berlin Wall coming down. But not too much. Len could probably have more fun without a wall.

The calls came in the next morning, two of them with a little urging. At Conferences International, the outfit that set up the computer links and interpreters, I hit the bull's-eye. Yes, Ms Hammond was an employee and yes, certainly, the message to call me would be passed on to her. I sat at my desk and thought about cigarettes and mid-morning drinking, two habits I'd reluctantly abandoned, while I waited for the call. As a result, I was edgy when the phone rang.

'Mr Hardy?' A crisp, businesslike female voice. A voice used to cutting through the shit and getting things done. 'This is Valerie Hammond. I'm returning your call.'

'I'll be honest with you, Ms Hammond. I'm a private investigator. It's not a legal matter. I'm working for Mr Robert Adamo. He hired me to locate you.'

'I see. And you've succeeded.'

'He needs to talk to you, very badly.'

The voice started off flat, dull almost, and rose in pitch and intensity, losing control. 'No. Positively not. Tell him I don't want to see him or talk to him. I don't want to marry him . . . or . . . or have children or have anything to do with him. Do you understand?'

'No,' I said.

'That's all. Leave me alone!' The line buzzed and then went dead; she must have fumbled cutting the connection. Very upset. Very intriguing. Very unsatisfactory. How do you tell a client you scored a bull's-eye but the arrow fell out of the target? You don't. I hung up and ran down the stairs and along the street to where my car was parked. I drove straight to the Conferences International office in Bent Street and parked almost outside. Totally illegal, but I didn't expect to be there long. I got out of the car and circled the tall building on foot—smoked glass windows, imposing entrance but no car park. I lounged in the street enjoying luxury again—I'd recognise her and she wouldn't know me from Harry M. Miller.

She came out fast, taller and blonder than I expected, but still Valerie H. as per the picture in my pocket. Her business clothes were smart and looked medium-expensive. No car. She stepped into a taxi, which had drawn up seconds before. The parking Nazi was just rounding the corner as I got back into my car and pulled away from the no parking zone. I jockeyed the Falcon into the traffic, a couple of cars behind the cab. I had my sunglasses on against the glare and a full tank of petrol; I had to hope that the driver was a sober type who signalled early and stopped for lights.

He was. The drive to Lindfield was almost sedate. I had no trouble keeping the cab in sight and staying unobtrusive myself. It was a little after eleven, with a fine, clear day shaping up. I squinted hard trying to read something from the woman's demeanour. She sat in the back the way most women passengers do. Nothing in that. She seemed to be sitting very rigidly, but it might have been my imagination. The cab turned off the main road just past the railway station and pulled up outside a small block of red-brick flats. For the area, very low-rent stuff. There was no mistaking her distress now; she rushed from the cab, leaving the door open, and almost fell as she plunged up the steps towards the small entrance.

Shaking his head, the cabbie got out, closed the door and drove away. I parked opposite the flats; the sun was shining directly through the windscreen and my shirt was sticking to my back. It was suddenly very hot and still. The highway was noisy, and I heard a train rattle past. This little patch of Lindfield seemed to have missed out on the trees and the quiet and the money. I sat in the car and looked at the flats. It didn't figure. Amy said she must be earning a bundle. Adamo said she had no vices. So why was she living here? Like other people in my racket, I've been known to trace someone, phone the client with the address and bank the cheque. Not this time. I had to know more.

It wasn't nearly as hot out of the car. I flapped my arms to unglue my shirt, and put on my jacket. A sticker over the letterbox told me that Hammond lived in Flat 3. That was one flight up, a narrow door at the top of a narrow set of stairs. Ratty carpet, cheap plastic screw-on numbers, flimsy handrail, no peephole, no buzzer. I knocked and held my licence folder at the ready. The door opened more quickly than I expected. A big man stood there. He was moon-faced, with thinning fair hair. He wore a white T-shirt and jeans that sagged under his bulging belly. He was well over 180 centimetres tall and must have weighed over ninety kilos, much of it fat.

'My name's Hardy,' I said. 'I'd like to see Ms Hammond.'

Valerie Hammond shrieked 'No,' from behind the fat man and he reacted by brushing the folder away, putting a big, meaty hand on my chest and pushing.

Fat can be a problem if it comes at you fast. This guy was serious, but he wasn't fast. I stepped back, surprised but balanced, and he swung a punch. I'd almost have had time to put my licence back in my pocket before it got anywhere near me. As it was, I moved to one side and let the punch drift away into thin air. That upset and angered him. He lowered his head and bullocked forward, trying to crush me against the brick wall a few feet back. Couldn't have that; I jolted the side of his head with a short elbow jab and pushed at him with my shoulder as he blundered past. He hit the wall awkwardly with his knee and head, groaned and went down.

I looked through the open door. Valerie Hammond was standing there with a shocked, dazed expression on her face. Her eyes were full of terror, and her hands were fluttering like lost birds. I couldn't think of a thing to say to her. I took out a card, bent and put it on the frayed carpet just inside the door. Behind me, the fat man was struggling gamely to his feet.

I pointed to the card. 'I don't mean you any harm. Robert Adamo is concerned about you. Call me when you feel calmer. I don't know what your trouble is, but maybe I can help. I didn't want to hurt this guy.'

Her hands stopped at her face, almost covering her eyes. I stepped clear of the man trying to make a grab at me and went down the stairs. I realised that I was breathing hard but not from the mild exertion. Valerie Hammond's fear had shaken me more than anything that Fatty could have done. I peeled off my jacket and sat sweating in the car, wondering what to do next. It was one of those times when the distress you run into seems to outweigh the distress of the person who hired you. It happens and it's confusing. The only way to cope is to get more information. I started the engine and drove away, grateful for the breeze created by the movement and feeling an overwhelming need for a drink.

I had the drink in a North Sydney pub and reviewed my options. All very well to want more information, but where to get it? I couldn't give a work-in-progress report to Adamo as things stood, and I didn't see Conferences International as a promising source. The only other person who'd dealt with the lady was Wesley, the taxi driver with the tuneful voice. *What the hell?* I thought. *He sounded bright, and she might have said something useful.* I had another glass of wine and a sandwich and rang Bernie at Redline, who told me that Wesley would be signing off at the depot about three o'clock. He'd tell Wesley I'd be there for a quick talk, but he warned me not to be late because Wesley would be buggered after his shift and wouldn't wait around.

Wesley was a Tongan, short and wide with a bushy black beard. He rubbed at the small of his back and flexed his shoulders as he spoke. 'Remember the lady well. Very upset, she was.'

'How d'you mean?'

'Crying. That's not so unusual there, you understand.'

'What? Where?'

'Where I picked her up—there in Mona Vale Road. Outside the place.'

'What place?'

'Some kind of institution for, you know, people with something wrong—mental cases, spastics and like that. Very sad place. But they treat them real good there. Looks very pricey—nice grounds, nurses in uniform, all that. But the visitors don't come away laughing. That all, brother? I'm bushed.'

I thanked him and Bernie and drove away with more questions in my mind but also some of the answers, maybe. I stopped at the post office in Glebe and located the Terrey Hills Nursing Clinic in Mona Vale Road in the phone book.

Then I called in at the surgery of Ian Sangster, who is a doctor and a friend, and a lover of intrigue. I waited while Ian disposed of two patients and then went into his light, airy consulting room. Ian is a jokester: he poured two measures of single malt whisky into medicine glasses and lifted his in a toast. 'Good health.'

We drank and I told him what I wanted.

'It's a top-class joint. Very good, very expensive. But it's for serious defectives, Cliff. I doubt you're ready for it yet.'

'You'll beat me to it if you keep knocking this stuff back the way you do,' I said. 'When will you know anything?'

'Tomorrow, late morning. I'll call you.'

That left me with another evening to kill. I went to a fitness centre in Balmain and hung around until someone turned up willing to play table tennis with me. The deal is, you hire one of the squash courts, a table, net and balls for an hour at an exorbitant price, and play as hard as you can to get your money's worth. I played against a police sergeant from the Balmain station and let him win, four matches to three. In my business, you never know when a friendly police sergeant might come in handy.

I went into the office in the morning, paid a few bills, requested payment for the third time from a faithless client and generally waited for Ian's

137

call. I plugged in a recording device and activated it when I heard Ian's voice on the line.

'Cliff,' he said. 'I've got good news and bad news. There's a patient named Carl Hammond who fills your bill. Aged twenty-three; the contact is his sister, Valerie Ursula . . .'

'That's it,' I said.

'Poor chap's in a very bad way.'

'What is it?'

'It's called kernicterus. This is the most severe case to come the way of the people there, and the worst I've ever heard of. Put simply, it's brain damage caused by jaundice at birth. The baby's red blood cells are broken down to such a degree that the liver can't cope with the by-products and this stuff called biliruben is released into the bloodstream. It's bile, essentially, a sort of stain that causes brain damage. Are you making notes or something?'

'I'm recording it, Ian. Go on.'

Sangster cleared his throat. 'Well, as I say, in a severe case a part of the brain is damaged and you get deafness, palsy, loss of coordination. Usually, in a case this bad, the baby is born prematurely and dies. That's called hydropis fetalis, for your information. Carl Hammond should have died. Some freak of nature kept him alive. A cruel freak, I'd call it. Not everyone would agree.'

'Can he . . .?'

'To almost any question you can put, the answer is no.'

138

'*Jesus.*'

'Not around when he was needed. I'm sorry, mate. This is grim stuff. He's there until he dies which could be tomorrow or ten years away. He requires complete care. The fees must be astronomical. Is that all you need?'

'Yes. No. What causes it?'

'The Rhesus factor.'

'What's that.'

'God, you laymen are so ignorant. No wonder we get so much money. It's an incompatibility between the mother's blood group and that of the foetus. The mother's metabolism sort of creates antibodies against the foetus, which pass through the placenta and fuck everything up. Get on to it early and you can do a transfusion and avoid the whole mess. Not in this case.'

'Why not?'

'Sorry. I don't know. It's a chance in a thousand sort of thing. Harder to detect twenty-odd years ago than now.'

I thanked him and rang off. I wound back the tape and played the conversation through again. Then I got out a dictionary and looked up some of the words while I made notes. I had an answer to one question now, at least—what Valerie Hammond did with her money. And, remembering her outcry on the phone, I had inklings of other questions and other answers. I resisted the impulse to go out for a drink before attempting to call Valerie Hammond. The only number I had

was at work. Maybe she hadn't gone in today.
I was almost hoping she hadn't when I heard
her voice, crisp and confidence-inspiring, on the
line.

'Valerie Hammond.'

She'd pulled herself together and sounded in
better emotional shape than me. But what do you
say? How do you tell someone you know their
secrets and their nightmares? I tried to keep my
voice level and calm, and I spoke very quickly.
'Ms Hammond, I don't want to distress you, but
I know about your brother and your problem.
I'm working for Mr Adamo, but I want to help
you. Please talk to me. Please don't hang up.'

I heard the sharp intake of breath, could sense
the struggle for control. 'I have to tell you I'm
taking Valium which is the only reason I'm able
to talk to you like this. What do you want, Mr
Hardy?'

'To talk to you for a few minutes, face to face.
If what I have to say doesn't make any sense to
you I'll back off, report to Mr Adamo that I couldn't
find you.'

'Very well. If it'll get rid of you. I don't mean
to be rude, but you're a violent man.'

'I'll meet you outside your office building. We
can talk as we walk. Play it by ear.'

'Did you follow me from work yesterday?'

Uncomfortable question, but it felt like time
to play everything straight with her. 'Yes. I hope
I didn't hurt your friend.'

'He's all right. He . . . he's just sharing the rent with me. It's an arrangement. I'm not . . . oh, what does it matter?'

This response was my first glimmer of hope; the first indication that she had some awareness of things outside the prison of her problems. 'In an hour, Ms Hammond?'

'Yes. I'll see you in an hour, Mr Hardy.'

She was on time and so was I. I walked up to her and we shook hands. It seemed like the right thing to do. She was wearing the same clothes she had on yesterday. So was I, as it happened. We walked along Bent Street past the government buildings, in the direction of the Stock Exchange. There were very few people about. We walked slowly. She said that she hoped this interview would be brief.

'Were you fond of Robert Adamo?' I asked.

'Very,' she said. 'Very, very fond. That was the trouble. I hadn't ever allowed myself to feel as much for anyone before. It was a mistake.'

'Why?'

'Robert wanted to marry me and for us to have children. I can't possibly do that, and you know why.' She quickened her pace slightly and spoke more quickly, as if she wanted to get the talk over. 'Oh, I know he loved me and he might have agreed not to have children. But that wouldn't have been fair on him. Or I might have weakened, or . . . or there might have been an accident. Anyway, my first duty is to Carl. I should never have got involved with Robert. He's too intense, too . . . good. His hiring you proves how serious he was. It was an awful, cruel thing for me to do.'

'I know this is painful for you, Ms Hammond, but I'd be glad if you could just answer a few questions. Why do you say you can't have children?'

Her high heels tapped faster. 'Because there is severe mental and physical disability in my genes.'

'Who told you that?'

'I didn't have to be told. Take a look at my brother, Mr Hardy.'

'Who told you?'

'My mother.'

'Did you ever inquire yourself about his condition, ask a doctor . . . ?'

'No. I love Carl, strange as it may seem. I just want to make sure he's as happy as he can be. That's all. That's my life.'

'When did your mother die?'

'Six years ago. She left Carl in my charge.'

We'd reached a row of benches outside a new steel and glass tower. I steered her towards one which was shaded by a tree growing in a large wooden box. 'Sit down, Ms Hammond.'

She sat. The tension in her body was visible in every line; also the slight buffer zone created by the Valium between her and the world. On close inspection, she was a little too heavy-featured to be really good-looking, but she was impressive and there was energy and intelligence behind her sadness. 'I can't imagine what you have to say to me,' she said.

'Your mother lied to you,' I said. 'I suppose she was afraid that if you led a full, normal life you'd neglect your brother. She told you a very cruel lie. Perhaps she was ashamed.'

'That's impossible! My mother was never ashamed of anything. She was . . . was immensely strong.'

'I imagine so. Nevertheless, the disability your brother suffers has nothing to do with genetics, at least as far as you're concerned.'

'What do you mean?'

I had to resort to my notes, but I pride myself that I gave it to her clearly and accurately. I explained the medical terms and stressed that the whole Rhesus tragedy could be easily averted by today's technology. She sat perfectly still and absorbed it all. Tears were running down her face by the time I'd finished. She pulled a tissue from her leather shoulder bag and blotted the tears. Through all the distress her mind was razor sharp. 'If what you say is true, how is it that I was born normal, and Carl had this terrible thing?'

'I'm not very sure of my ground here,' I said. 'It could be a matter of chance, but if not, I think you know the answer.'

'Different fathers?'

I nodded. 'And the reason for your mother's behaviour. Guilty people can be strong and vice versa. When did your father die?'

'A few years after Carl was born. They were very unhappy, my mother and father. They fought terribly. I was very young and didn't understand much. I thought it was because of Carl, or the money. But perhaps . . .'

She was sobbing now. I put my arm around her shoulders, and she rested her head against me. 'You've got a lot to think about,' I said. 'Most of it's very painful, but not all. You don't have to think of yourself as cursed or tainted. I don't want to push things, but Adamo's a good man. I don't see many, but I recognise one when I do. I think you'd find him understanding and sympathetic . . .'

She lifted her head and sniffed. 'He's very smart, too, isn't he?'

I remembered Adamo's firmness of purpose, his confidence that he could set things right if he just got a little help. 'Smart enough to run a small business profitably,' I said. 'I'm here to tell you that's tough. And smart enough to be in love with you and to hire me. Yes, I'd say he's pretty bright.'

The House of Ruby

'Good afternoon, sir,' the woman behind the table said. 'My name is Marcia. Do you want someone in particular, or a special service?'

'In a way,' I said. 'I'd like to see Ruby.'

Marcia was a nice-looking woman, thirtyish, with short curly hair and a humorous expression. The fact that her ruffled blouse was open almost to the waist and her make-up would have looked garish out of the dim orange light was to be expected. This was The House of Ruby, massage parlour and relaxation centre in Darlinghurst Road, Kings Cross, and the woman behind the table wasn't selling raffle tickets. She pressed a red button on the desk. The blue button, I knew, summoned two or three women in various states of undress. The red one, appropriately, summoned Ruby.

'Cliff, my love, you came.'

'Once or twice, Ruby,' I said. 'It's good to see you looking so well.'

Ruby is about fifty, and carries a lot of flesh on a large frame, but she carries it with style.

Her hair is red and luxuriant, like her lipstick. She was wearing a purple silk dress that outlined her charms rather than displayed them. The dress was short, however; Ruby has great legs and them she displays. She reached for me with her ruby-ringed fingers and red-painted nails. 'Just you come in here, love, and I'll give you a drink and tell you a story that'll make you weep.'

'Private eyes don't weep,' I said.

Ruby burst into laughter, and I heard the woman behind the desk snigger a little too. Definitely the place to go to be appreciated for your wit, Ruby's. She took me through a door and down a short passage to her private suite, which is fitted out like an erotic dream—silk and velvet hangings, black and red decor, pornographic paintings and photographs. Ruby poured generous measures of scotch into tall glasses and added ice. 'Put you in the mood, Cliff?'

'Sure,' I said. 'But it's just a bit overdone. I kind of get out of the mood from having been put in the mood, if you follow.'

She nodded. 'Me too, but it's what the punters like.'

I lifted my glass and drank down some good, nicely iced scotch. 'How's Kathy?'

'Fine. Two kids.'

Kathy was Ruby's daughter, who I'd found one time after she'd run off on learning that her mother was a whore and a madam. Kathy was a convent-educated teenager at the time, and I'd taken her back to my place, where my tenant, Hilde Stoner, and I had talked to her for several days about life and the world. I'd shown her a bit of it, in the Cross and around Darlinghurst, and she got a different perspective on things. She'd been her mother's greatest supporter ever since, and Ruby was a friend of mine for life. I could've fucked my brains out for free forever if I'd been that way inclined. As it was, I'd availed myself of Ruby's services but twice, in moments of distress.

'So, what's the problem, Ruby?' I said. 'The girl out front looks nice—you seem to be keeping up your usual standards. Are you still catering to the taste for older women?'

Ruby drank deeply, which was a worrying sign; she usually sipped for a while and then forgot she had a drink. 'Of course. Best decision I ever made. You get a better class of client and a more mature employee—less trouble all round. And Marcia out there? She's the best. Professional woman, in the true sense of the word. She's a doctor, would you believe? Runs a small practice part-time and does an elegant job here as well.'

'So what is it? AIDS? Fred Nile picketing you?'

She waved her hand dismissively; the red stones in her rings glittered. 'AIDS. Nonsense. As safe here as in Turramurra. Safer. Not that it hasn't hurt business. All the publicity, I mean. But no, nothing like that. Sammy Weiss's trying to put the squeeze on me.'

147

'Sammy? Never.'

'Can you believe it? He owns the building, or most of it. I know that, and he knows that I know. So I pay him rent, on a lease. Fine.'

'He's putting up the rent?'

'No. He wants a percentage of my earnings, and he wants it to appear on the books as rent. He's negatively geared all over the bloody place. It's no skin off his arse, but I simply can't afford it. Not a hike of two hundred per cent.'

I'd been sinking down in my velvet chair a little, lulled by the scotch and thinking the story wouldn't have much bite. Now I sat up. 'You mean double?'

'No, I do not mean double.' Ruby finished her drink in a swallow. 'I don't know what I mean. All I know is he wants the rent to go this month up by as much again as it is now and by that much again next month. What's that? He calls it two hundred per cent.'

'I'd call it treble,' I said.

'I call it ruin. Will you talk to him, Cliff? I pay that and I've got to run this place like a cattleyard—use kids, junkies, all that shit. I'd rather close up, and that'd put some decent women out of work. And I'm helping Kathy's husband get started as a nurseryman. I've got commitments. You know Sammy. I can't think what's got into him. He used to be a reasonable guy. Will you talk to him, Cliff? Please? I'm asking as a friend, and I'm paying. This is a business expense.'

I didn't like to see Ruby knocking back the scotch as if she needed it, or the desperation in her eyes, so I said I'd talk to Sammy. That night I had nothing much else to do after I'd finished escorting a big gambler from the club in Edgecliff to the night safe in Woollahra, so I went looking for Sammy. Night is the only time to see him; that's when he eats dinner at the Jack Daniels Bar 'n' Grill and pays visits to several strip joint nightclubs in which he has an interest. What he does in the daytime I don't know—sleeps or counts money, maybe both.

I found him in the Skin Cellar, a sleazoid hole in the wall around the corner from one of his classier joints in the Cross. The place was crowded, and the clientele was drunk and rowdy and giving the pre-owned blonde on the pocket-handkerchief stage a bad time.

'Get 'em off!'

'If I can't touch 'em, I don't believe 'em.'

'Shake it, gran'ma!'

The music howled deafingly, a clatter of drums and electric machines. Through the smoke I spotted Sammy sitting at a table with two other men. This was normal. Sammy has a wife named Karen, pronounced Kah-ren, who keeps him on a tight, monogamous leash. What wasn't normal was the reaction of one of Sammy's companions as I pushed my way through the smoke and the drunken lurching that passed for dancing. He pushed back his chair and stood—thin and dark

like me, but 188 centimetres, giving him that uncomfortable two and a half centimetre advantage
and with an acne-eaten face to back it up.

'This guy's carrying, Sammy,' he grated.

Observant. I had my licensed Smith & Wesson
.38 under my arm, the way the nervous winning
gambler liked it. I nodded at Sammy, hoping to
bypass the heavy, but he wasn't buying it. I saw
the fist just before it hit me and ducked. I hadn't
had a drink since midafternoon at Ruby's, or I
might have been too slow. As it was, I had the
adrenalin edge: I let the punch go past and hacked
at the guy's shins with my right shoe. I connected
and he yelped. He was reaching inside his jacket
for something serious when I clipped him on the
chin with a half-serious left hook. He was moving
the wrong way, into the punch, and it snapped
his neck back. That kind of pain makes you think
about giving up, and he did. He slumped to the
floor and I reached inside his coat, expecting to
find a gun. Instead, my fingers closed over the
handle of a chunky flick-knife held in a spring-
loaded holster. I pulled it out, sprung the blade
and dropped the knife on the floor. I brought
my heel down hard on it.

'Sammy,' I said, 'what the hell d'you think you're
playing at?'

'Don't move a muscle, shithead,' a heavily ac-
cented voice said close to my ear. I smelled
sweat and aftershave. The other man at the table
had slid away and come up behind me while

acne-scars had been doing his thing. I stood very
still because I could feel something digging into
my right kidney and I knew it wasn't a broom
handle. He dug the gun in some more and then
moved it away. Professional. You know it's there,
but you don't know precisely where. And it was
no good thinking, *He won't kill me, not in a public
place.* Above that racket a shot from a small calibre
pistol wouldn't be heard, and a bullet in the leg
is not a laughing matter.

'Sammy,' I said, 'this isn't your style.'

But Sammy Weiss seemed to be enjoying himself. His smooth, pasty face, normally fairly good-
natured as long as things were going his way,
was set in a scowl that he seemed to have grown
used to. Sammy had put on weight since I'd last
seen him, and lost some hair. But he was more
snappily dressed and more carefully groomed—
silk tie, shirt with a discreet stripe, lightweight
double-breasted suit.

He snapped his fingers and his buffed nails
gleamed briefly. 'Toss him out, Turk. Don't do
no damage but, he's got a nasty nature.'

'Sammy . . .'

The pistol dug back in again, and the man I'd
dropped was starting to get to his feet. Turk had
all the moves; he jerked my elbow around, and
you have to give when that happens. He prodded
again and I found myself pushing through the
crowd towards the door. I was confused by
Sammy's behaviour, but not completely thrown.

Before we got to the door I sidestepped and watched Turk move automatically in the same direction. I dug my knee into his balls and reached for the gun, but he'd put it away and my move threw me a little off-balance. He recovered fast and stepped back—a medium-sized, dark guy, strongly built with a bald head and a thick, compensatory moustache. Stand-off. People were starting to notice us now.

'See you again, Turk,' I said.

He spat at my feet and backed away into the crowd.

I was still mulling it over the next morning— the change in Sammy Weiss from lair businessman who liked to flirt with the rough element to crime boss with minders—when Sammy's brother, Benjamin, knocked and walked into my office.

'I heard what happened last night, Cliff.'

'I hope you heard it right, Benjamin,' I said. No-one ever called him Benny. He was an accountant, very straight.

'I heard there was a gun and a knife. Sammy's lost his mind.' He put his hat on my desk, lowered his small, neat body into a chair and ran a tired hand across his worried face. Benjamin is older, smaller and quieter; the brothers look alike only around the eyes, where intelligence is suggested.

'That's how it looked to me. What's going on?'

'First, would you mind telling me what you wanted to see him about?'

That's Benjamin, always getting the figures in the columns first. I told him about Ruby and Sammy.

'That's a good, steady business. The property's being well cared for, and it's appreciating. Things being the way they are, Ruby could probably handle a modest rent hike, but nothing like this.'

'I agree. What's got into your brother?'

'He's a changed man. Dresses differently, struts around with those two hoods. He's drinking and gambling more, acting the big shot. But all this is so heavy-handed, dealing with you and Ruby like that. If he tries it on the wrong people . . .' Benjamin shook his head and looked even more worried.

I knew what he meant. There were people in Sydney who'd take Sammy and Turk and the other guy apart just for fun. 'There must be a reason,' I said. 'A woman?'

'Come on. You know what sort of chain Karen keeps him on. No, I guess he's just bored. That plus the piece that appeared in *Sydney Scene* about him.'

'You've got me.'

'It's an insignificant little shoestring mag, run by a couple of queers. They did an article on Sydney's crime czars and somehow Sammy got a mention and a quote. Now he thinks he's Mr Big.'

'Jesus. That's dangerous.'

Benjamin leaned forward in his chair. 'I love Sammy, Cliff. He's a good man basically, always been very generous with me. He's a good husband and father. I don't want to see him get into trouble. Could you . . .'

'Hold on. We're talking conflict of interest here.'

'I don't see why.' His small hands came up and he started ticking points off on his fingers. 'One, Ruby wants Sammy off her back; two, I want Sammy to wake up to himself; three, you'd like to get your own back on Turk.'

'Who says so?'

Benjamin smiled. 'I know you, Cliff.'

I thought about it, but not for long. I had to admit it was an interesting problem. Tough, but not too tough. And I had an affection for Sammy which dated back to the days of the Victoria Street green bans, when he was on the side of the angels. Good business, as it turned out: he made money on his houses in the street. Still. 'What're Sammy's weaknesses?' I asked.

Benjamin didn't need his fingers. 'First, he's afraid of Karen; second, he's a hypochondriac.'

'That's interesting. Who's his doctor?'

'He never goes near them. He doses himself for his imagined illnesses. He tells me about them all the time, but I'm sure he's as healthy as a horse. So far.'

'Leave it with me, Benjamin, along with a couple of hundred bucks. I'll see if I can work something out.'

Benjamin wrote me a cheque. I gave him a receipt. He put on his hat and went, leaving me to do some thinking, of which two hundred dollars buys a fair bit.

Marcia was behind the table when I dropped in at Ruby's that afternoon. She had on another plunging blouse, and I had the feeling that the parts of her body I couldn't see weren't warmly clothed either.

'Ruby?' she said.

'No. I'd like to talk to you, doctor.'

She smiled, and I could see humorous lines under the make-up. 'Ruby's been chattering. I have to say she cheered up a bit after she saw you yesterday. She's been very down.'

'Do you know why?'

She shook her head and the jaunty, short hair bounced. 'No. This is an excellent establishment, and business seems to be good. You're not a policeman, are you?'

'Private enquiries. My name's Cliff Hardy.'

It surprised us both that we shook hands.

'What do you want to talk to me about?'

For the second time that day I told the story of Ruby's troubles. This time there was a second strand—the metamorphosis of Sammy Weiss. Marcia listened intently, asking one or two questions. We had to break once while she dealt with a customer—for Henrietta and the special—but when I finished I felt as if I'd clarified a few things for myself as well as shared the problem with a good thinker.

'I like Ruby very much,' Marcia said. 'And I want to help. How can I? You haven't told me this for nothing.'

'You practise somewhere? You've got a surgery?'

'Hardly that. The front room of a terrace in Stanley Street.'

'That'll do. Is there something we could slip Sammy to give him the symptoms of a venereal disease—fever, discharge and so on?'

She took a deep, very distracting breath. I tried to sneak a look at her legs under the table. Well, it was that kind of a situation. 'Yes, there is,' she said. 'Cantharides'd do it.'

'What's that?'

'Spanish fly. Take enough, and you feel you're pissing razor blades.'

'What about . . . discharge?'

She shook her head. 'Harder. Massive vitamin C'd produce stains.'

'But no serious damage.'

She shook her head. 'Not in the short term.'

'How does it come, this stuff?'

'Granules. They're rather bitter.'

'Sammy has a couple of long blacks with his brother every morning and after work.'

'Three days,' Marcia said. 'Four at the most.'

I spoke to Benjamin in his office, which was a flat in a pre-war building in Riley Street, another of Sammy's holdings.

'A doctor and she's a whore? What's the world coming to?'

'Tell yourself it's getting more interesting,' I said. 'It works for me. All you have to do is slip this stuff into Sammy's espresso. Couple of days later you tell him he's looking terrible and offer to help. Make sure he takes a lot of vitamin C. Be subtle. If that doesn't work, be direct.'

Benjamin agreed to do it. Three days later he was on the phone to me. 'Sammy's desperate,' he said. 'I can't bear to see it. What's next?'

I gave him the telephone number and the address in Stanley Street.

'How am I supposed to know these symptoms?'

I'd done some checking on Benjamin in the quiet hours. It's always wise to check on a co-conspirator. There was more to him than met the eye. He had a personal interest in some of Sammy's assets, and he was not unknown at The House of Ruby. 'Benjamin,' I said, 'if your wife is the only woman you've ever shtupped, I'm a Dutchman.'

He disposed of that with a quiet cough. I repeated the address and told him not to worry. He called me at home that night.

'Tomorrow at 2.00 p.m., as planned,' he said.

'Good. Will he be alone?'

'Of course. You think he wants anyone to know about this? What's the matter, Cliff? Are you afraid of Turk?' It was the first time I'd heard an edge on Benjamin's voice since this business began.

157

I was glad of it; it meant that he wanted Sammy straightened out as much as my other client did.

'Turk'll come later,' I said. 'Let's get this done first.'

Sammy turned up in a taxi at Marcia's terrace five minutes early. He was as nervous as a schoolboy buying condoms; he glanced up and down the street and then stared at the house. That must have been a comfort: Marcia's place had a neat, tiled frontage, just the right amount of greenery and a confidence-inspiring brass knocker. I was watching from the balcony. Sammy knocked. I scurried down the stairs and took up my position with the camera behind the screen in the front room. Marcia, wearing a short skirt, very high heels and a starched white lab coat, jotted down Sammy's details on a card. She arched a plucked eyebrow once, presumably at some blatant lie of Sammy's. I was alarmed; although her make-up was much toned down for the event, I was afraid she might overdo things. She didn't. Her instruction to Sammy to take off his pants was clinical. Sammy was so embarrassed he shut his eyes when she examined him. This allowed Marcia to open the lab coat. I had the silent camera whirring the whole time: Sammy's flaccid dick in Marcia's hands, the lacquered nails showing clearly; Marcia, her breasts dropping forward out of a lacy black bra under the starched white fabric and her hand clasped around Sammy's balls; Sammy, bent over, his underpants around his ankles, and Marcia behind him with the coat shrugged back on her shoulders, muscular thighs showing under the mini-skirt and her rubber-gloved finger probing Sammy's arsehole.

'Get dressed, Mr Jones,' Marcia said.

Sammy did, with relief. Marcia stripped off the gloves, washed her hands in a bowl and dried them on a white towel. Sammy sat on a plastic chair. I could see the sweat standing out around his receding hairline. Marcia picked up Sammy's card and made a few notes. She'd buttoned up the lab coat and assumed a prim, professional expression.

'Well, doctor?' Sammy said.

'You have nothing to worry about, Mr Jones. Your condition is the result of a dietary irregularity—lack of calcium, principally. Do you drink much milk?'

The gratitude and pleasure on Sammy's face was childlike. 'Never touch the stuff.'

'You've built up an imbalance in your body chemistry. I recommend milk and goat's cheese, also green vegetables. As much as you can get down.' Marcia scribbled on a prescription pad.

'Sure thing. And . . .?' Sammy said.

Marcia tore off the sheet. 'These pills. Twice a day before meals.'

'You mean three times a day.'

'No. Skip lunch. You should eat only a light breakfast and a high calcium dinner. No meat.'

'Pasta?'

'Light on the oil.'

Sammy jumped to his feet and thrust his manicured hand at Marcia's middle. 'Thank you, doctor. Thank you.'

'Here's your prescription. Have you got your Medicare card?'

'Let's make it cash,' Sammy said.

Benjamin and I had agreed that there was no point in lying, no working through go-betweens. We didn't want Sammy worried out of his mind. I arrived at Benjamin's office by arrangement late the following day to find the two brothers drinking coffee. Sammy said it was the first decent coffee he'd had in days. Benjamin didn't say anything. Sammy was expansive and ready to apologise for our misunderstanding of a few nights back.

I cut him off and spread the photographs out on the desk beside his coffee cup. I'm no artist of the lens, but the pictures were eloquent enough. Marcia looked delicious in her unfastened coat, Sammy's closed eyes could be taken for transports of ecstasy, and so on. Sammy looked at the photos and slowly reddened from his soft chin to his retreating hairline. He looked across the desk at Benjamin and his eyes were moist.

'You set me up. Your own brother.'

'It was for your own good, Samuel. Believe me, your own good, and mine and everybody's.'

'Your own brother.'

'I'm not your brother, Sammy,' I said, 'but I am your friend, or I can be if you play ball.'

'What's the rules?' Sammy said softly.

Benjamin got up and took the coffee pot off the warmer. He poured some more into Sammy's cup and filled a cup for me.

'First, you lay off Ruby. Leave her rent alone, don't hassle her in any way. Meet any reasonable requests she has as a good tenant.'

'And?'

'You stop pissing around with hoods like Turk. Stop acting the big shot.'

'Attend to business,' Benjamin said.

I sipped some of the terrific coffee. 'Exactly.'

'Or?' Sammy said.

'I take the pictures to Karen along with the doctor's report on you—that you presented for a suspected venereal disease and so on.'

Sammy snarled, 'Doctor!'

I said, 'She *is* a doctor, Sammy, and she gave you the straight goods. There's nothing wrong with you. You took a few doses of Spanish fly, which caused you a few temporary problems. That's all.'

The cloud that had been gathering on Sammy's brow lifted. 'You mean it? That woman really is a doctor?'

'Sure,' I said. 'I just got your urine tests back. You're clean.'

Sammy drank his coffee in one gulp. The flush in his face receded and he grinned. Then he exploded into laughter. 'You guys,' he said. 'You fuckin' guys. You finally get me to go to a doctor. Me, scared shitless of doctors. And I'm OK?'

I nodded. 'Sound as a bell. Sammy, while you're laughing, I can't quite see why you were worried. I mean, you haven't stepped out of line, have you?'

Sammy looked at his brother. 'You knew, didn't you?'

Benjamin nodded. 'I knew the scheme'd work, Cliff. Sammy worries about toilet seats, mosquitoes, knives and forks in restaurants . . .'

'You can catch things,' Sammy chuckled as he spoke.

It was time to cut through the hilarity. 'Okay, Sammy,' I said. 'I'm glad you're happy. We did you a favour, fine. But the terms still apply. Get ahold of yourself, or Karen makes your life a living hell. I don't need to spell it out, do I?'

Sammy shook his head; suddenly glumness enveloped him. 'It's not that easy.'

'How so?' Benjamin said.

Sammy waved his hand and it was almost as if he was saying goodbye to buffed nails and shaped cuticles. 'It's Turk,' he said. 'He's kinda . . . pressing me. You know?'

'Don't worry about Turk,' I said.

A little checking turned up something odd and interesting about Turk. He didn't have a permanent place of residence; instead, he moved around a circuit of city hotels, staying two weeks or three weeks at a time in one place after another. Not five-star hotels, but not fleapits either. The sorts of places I like to stay in myself, and where I stick out-of-town clients. Spending some money on the street and using the phone, I located his current hostelry, the Sullivan in Elizabeth Street, where I happened to know the security man.

Bert Loomis is an ex-cop, ex-bank security man, ex quite a few things. He's fifty-five and looks every minute of it, especially around the eyes, which have seen most of the dirty things there are to see. I judged that $50 would be about right, and it was.

'Fifteen minutes, Hardy,' Loomis said. I noticed that he didn't touch the knob, just slipped the card in the slot and edged the door open with his knee.

'Right,' I said. 'Where'll you be?'

'Nowhere.'

He jerked his head; I went into the suite and heard the door close behind me. I had to work fast, and Turk made it easy. He lived light—basic toilet articles in the bathroom, clothes in the closet and drawers. Condoms, a vibrator and pornographic material in a bedside cabinet. Beer and wine in the bar fridge, hard liquor on top. Two suitcases, empty. Dirty clothes in a heap in the corner of the little balcony room that overlooked the park. The drawer in the solid writing desk was locked and the Sullivan didn't run to a security safe for guests. I picked the lock and emptied the drawer out on the bed. Personal papers, money matters—bank books, chequebooks, statements, bills from a firm of accountants, three passports.

I checked my watch. Twelve minutes. Time was up. I turned on the radio and dumped a drawer full of underwear onto the floor, where it could be seen from the doorway. Then I moved across to the door, opened it and left it propped open with the toe of one of Turk's high-heeled boots. According to the passports, Konstanides/Lycos/Mahoud measured 183 centimetres—he'd looked taller in the Skin Cellar and the boots explained why. I stood inside the bathroom, two metres from the doorway, with my .38 Smith & Wesson at the ready. I was there because I knew Bert Loomis couldn't resist a doublecross or a dollar.

Turk was quiet, but I could sense and smell him. He edged through the door, and I could imagine him standing in the short hallway, hearing the radio, looking at the mess on the floor. I could feel his tension. I stepped out with the .38 levelled at 150 centimetres. Turk was fast: he saw me, ducked, pulled out his own gun and came on. But the round hole staring at him had held his attention for just long enough, and I had the advantages of height and readiness; I moved aside, reached forward and clubbed his bald head with my metal-loaded fist. The barrel and trigger guard tore his skin, and the blow almost stunned him. His knees gave and I chopped at his right wrist, bringing my left hand down hard and bunched. He dropped his gun. I hit him between the eyes with my left and felt the knuckles protest. He fell forward and I kneed him in the chest as he came down.

After that, there was no fight in him. I pulled him into the bedroom and bound his ankles and wrists with four striped silk neckties from his closet. Bert Loomis put his head through the door, and I pointed my gun at him and he went away. Then I called the Immigration Department's investigations branch and told them I had an illegal immigrant in custody—an individual with multiple passports, multiple bank accounts, several driver's licences and a concealed weapon.

I had a beer from Turk's fridge while I waited for the Immigration boys. Turk and I didn't speak. I showed them the documents and Turk's gun, and there wasn't a whole lot more to say. Turk's eyes blazed at me as they read him his rights and put the cuffs on.

'You shouldn't have spat at me, Turk,' I said as they packed up his belongings. 'I really didn't like it at all.'

Sammy Weiss was as relieved to get Turk off his back as he was to learn that he didn't have the pox or anything else. All he had to worry about was the photos, and I set his mind at rest about them.

'All you have to do, Sammy,' I said, 'is leave Ruby alone and behave yourself. Listen to Benjamin, do what he says. In six months, if you toe the line, I'll give you the pictures.'

We were in the Bar Calabria, drinking coffee. Sammy was wearing a quiet suit and tie and looking hurt. 'You don't trust me.'

'How do you spell it?' I said. 'Deal?'

'Deal. Really a doctor, huh?'

Benjamin was pleased and insisted on paying me over and above the two hundred retainer. He offered to do any accounting I needed free of charge. Ruby paid me as well—a couple of days work, and expenses, such as my payment to Marcia, and for film and developing. It was a nice piece of business. After I'd collected the cheque and a drink and an enthusiastic kiss from Ruby, I stopped at the table by the door. Marcia was painting her nails and reading the *Independent Monthly*.

'You were great,' I said. 'Thanks.'

She looked up and blew on a wet nail. 'My pleasure. Anything else I can do for you?'

Almost Wedded Bliss

Reasons to remember 1967—the release of *Sergeant Pepper*, the Six Day War, the hanging of Ronald Ryan, the drowning of Harold Holt. I remember it because that was the year Astrid and I nearly got married.

My life had been going along in two and three-year zigs and zags—two years in the army, two years at university, three as an insurance claims investigator. I had a flat in North Sydney and I was doing all right—people were always burning things down and cheating in various ways that needed to be uncovered to protect the other people who played the game straight. That was how I looked at it. I had energy to burn and I straightened out certain problems for friends. I also did an occasional bit of bodyguarding on the side, like for the 1966 Bob Dylan tour, although I never got closer than twenty feet to the man himself.

I met Astrid in early '67 at an anti-Vietnam rally. I was along for the ride, to see if any of the speakers and rallyers knew what they were talking about. Some did. Astrid was tall and thin and blonde and she stood out in a fairly unwashed crowd like a swan among ducks. Like most people, she was surprised to learn that the war I'd fought in, the Malayan Emergency, had ended only seven years before. I had scars, cynicism and experience. She had enthusiasm, idealism and a thirst for knowledge. She was from Wahroonga—selective high school, Fine Arts degree from Sydney; I was from Maroubra, suburb and school, University of New South Wales drop-out. She worked for a publisher. I read the odd book. A perfect match.

She moved into my flat and we had a big party because Astrid was saying goodbye to her North Shore origins. Her widowed mother and my sister got along fine. Our friends, hers from the university and the publishing game, mine from the army, two cops and Clem Carter who went to gaol soon after although he was innocent, did likewise. A good party. We even went off to the Blue Mountains for a sort of non-honeymoon and then it was back to work. Busy lives, dynamite sex on the pill, boozy Italian dinners. A kind of trial marriage. A magic time.

The first non-routine job that came along after I took up with Astrid was weird from the jump. A man named Lawrence Bean, who'd been referred to me by a man I'd saved from going to prison by proving he hadn't torched his factory, arrived at the flat with a proposition. He operated a nightclub off Darlinghurst Road. 'It's going to be the top R 'n' R spot in the Cross,' he said.

'Rock 'n' Roll?'

He laughed and shook his head. He was a small man, about fifty, with hair that waved tightly back across his bat-eared skull. He had a Jimmy Durante nose in danger of becoming a W.C. Fields. He was a constant, nervy smoker. I was a smoker myself in those days, rolling them, using them to relax and as an aid to thought. Lawrie, as he insisted on being called, used them to fuel some inner fire.

'No, mate. Haven't you heard? The Yanks are coming! Rest and Recreation. The town's going to be full of GIs with greenbacks to burn.'

I'd heard about it, in a vague sort of a way, but it hadn't meant much to me. It had happened before, in the Second World War, and the country had survived, although there'd been some casualties—the women strangled in the Melbourne 'brown out' murders, a few soldiers killed in brawls, the good-time girls who were the victims of botched abortions. We were all more sophisticated now. What was the problem?

Lawrie mashed out his Rothmans and lit another immediately. 'My place is called the Rocky Mountain Bar.'

'Cosmopolitan,' I said.

He ignored that. 'I've got American beers—Pabst Blue Label, Budweiser, Schlitz—you name it.'

'Lone Star,' I said.

'Huh? Never mind. You see my point. When those thirsty fighting boys, so far from home, get here they're going to find familiar bottles and, if you'll excuse the joke, familiar women. Hah hah.'

'Hah,' I said. 'Rough guessing your mark-up, Lawrie, but I'd say you're about to become a very rich man.'

He sucked gloomily on the Rothmans. 'I thought so, too. Until I started getting trouble from someone who should be doing the same thing himself. Shit, there's enough in this for everyone. Do you know how much those poor bastards . . . those brave boys, get paid?'

I shook my head. Everything was more casual in those days, remember. You wrote fewer things down, took what money you could in cash, worried less about rules and regulations. Astrid was proving expensive and my salary was being stretched. 'Get to the point, Lawrie.'

'There's a pub opposite my place called the Macquarie, maybe you know it?'

'I've seen it.'

'Bloke who's taken it over is doing it up—new carpet, paint job, lights. That'd be OK, improve the tone, 'cept this bloke's an army nut. He's going to fit one of the bars out like an army mess—flags all over the fuckin' place, ANZAC shit. Aussie servicemen'll get drinks half-price on Friday and Saturday night. Now d'you see the point?'

I did. Australian and American troops have never

mixed well—something to do with different national images, the sociologists say. An American private saluting a colonel feels honoured, an Australian private doesn't. He'll look the other way if he can. That's part of it, but there're simpler things. Australians resent the Yanks' equipment, diet and pay. The extra pay means extra alcohol and sex—put all those things together and you see the problem at the operational level. Two bars in close proximity, catering to similar needs on unequal terms, spelled trouble.

'Could get lively,' I said.

'Could get fuckin' murderous,' Bean said. 'I was in Brisbane in '44 when we took them on. Jesus, it was nearly as bad as the *real* war, I'm telling you.'

I nodded. I'd heard stories of the Brisbane street battles between Australian and American soldiers from one of my uncles. 'I can see the problem, Lawrie. But what do you want me to do? I'm not the captain of a team of bouncers.'

Lawrie's next Rothmans was a stub between his dark-brown fingers. 'I want you to talk to the guy at the Macquarie,' he said. 'I'm told he's a mate of yours—Ken Barraclough.'

Captain Ken Barraclough. Just hearing his name took me out of the flat straight back to Malaya where the light in the jungle played tricks so that shadows moved, and the only thing hotter and wetter than the air was your skin. Barraclough was first our instructor in camp, then our CO in

171

the field. He drummed his motto—'Kill and Survive'—into us with his fists, boots and shouts. That first week of training was torture—inching slowly through swamps, sprinting across clearings, climbing, crawling, scrambling—with booby traps showering stinking mud and stinging stones. He woke us up at 2.00 a.m. for refinements like flame-thrower attacks, and browbeat and punished us until every man in the company could hold his breath under water for two minutes and climb a forty-foot rope with a full pack.

We hated him worse than the enemy, feared him more, and so became death and survival machines like himself. His training saved my life a dozen times and won me a field commission. Then the politicians declared it was all over and we were going home. I got drunk and attempted to thank him. It was unthinkable to try it sober. He was drunk, too, we all were. He looked at me and his black moustache twitched and he said, 'I never picked you for a poofter, Hardy.'

I'd heard nothing of him since then. His name came up when I had a drink with army mates, but no-one seemed to know what had become of him. Barraclough wasn't the sort of man you kept in touch with.

I rolled a smoke, remembering how quickly you had to do that in Malaya if you didn't want it to get soggy. 'What makes you think me and Barraclough are mates?'

'He's got this fuckin' photo up in the pub. "A"

Company piss-up. My mate, the bloke you helped out, recognised your ugly mug.'

I didn't recall a photograph being taken, but I could visualise the picture—all cockeyed smiles and glassy eyes. All except Barraclough, who could drink all night and not get a hair out of place. 'I can't imagine Ken Barraclough running a pub,' I said. 'He's not exactly the sociable type.'

'You're telling me. I went to see him, friendly like, and asked him to tone down the Digger stuff. He'd have tossed me out on my ear if he could have.'

I looked Bean over again. An unimpressive physical specimen to start with, he'd done further damage with tobacco and booze. The Ken Barraclough I knew could've thrown him from one side of Darlinghurst Road to the other. Bean saw me looking and read my mind.

'Poor bugger's got no fuckin' legs,' he said.

I agreed to talk to Barraclough, although I was already suspecting that something strange was going on. I took some money from Lawrie and got rid of him before Astrid got home with her manuscripts that we laughed at and attempted one of her laughable meals that usually ended up in the kitchen tidy. Mostly we drank wine and ate bread and cheese and eggs. Great fun. The next day I went off to perform the chores I got paid for. The alarm system, installed in the house of

173

a very nervous bookie in Double Bay, was adequate; the solicitor, who'd tried to pay his premiums with a bad cheque, was argumentative. I threatened him with cancellation and penalty fees and he became more reasonable. Which brought me to 6.30 p.m. in Homebush. The end of a long, warm day with my private work on the south side of the harbour still to do. I rang Astrid and told her I wouldn't be back to eat.

'Why not?' she said.

'I've got this job to do, at the Cross.'

That produced a silence. You have to understand that this was 1967 and Astrid, for all her liberation, was still a North Shore girl. Kings Cross meant only one thing to her—commercial sex.

'Oh?'

I tried to explain something of it to her, but that only made things worse. The conversation ended coolly—upsetting when you've only been together a few weeks. I drove to Darlinghurst, ate something in an Italian restaurant and drank some red wine. About nine o'clock I wandered through the Cross and turned into the street that accommodated the Macquarie Hotel and the Rocky Mountain Bar. It was Friday night and the Cross was busy—girls on the street, pubs noisy and plenty of punters about. A few in uniform. Australia didn't have a lot of hippies in those days, but what we had were mostly to be found in places like the Cross. The cops eyed the long-haired men and the bare-footed women in long skirts with more suspicion than the whores and bikies.

The pub and the bar across the street were doing business, although both bore signs of renovation still going on. The neon Stars and Stripes outside the Rocky Mountain wasn't lit, and the Macquarie's Digger Bar featured a backlit, giant-sized rising sun badge that was flickering faintly. Some bugs still in the electrics. I went down a set of steps under the badge into a space that smelled of beer and tobacco. But the smells were fresh, warring with the odours of new carpet and fresh paint.

The place was a cross between an army mess and a conventional Australian pub. There was a fair bit of military insignia scattered around—crossed .303s mounted over the bar, a big reproduction of Dyson's portrait of Simpson and his donkey, regimental flags. Lots of photographs. There was a light fug in the bar and I had to squint to make out the details of the photo on the wall beside the Gents. The faces were all familiar—WO Ron Herbert, Frank Harper, Alby Abbott, the RSM. Ken Barraclough was in the middle of the group, scowling, glass in hand, looking as if he wished he were on parade. I was on his left, lighting a cigarette. I rolled one now as I gazed at a piece of my own history.

A flame flared inches from my face. 'Light, Hardy?'

I looked down. Barraclough had run his wheel-chair up silently, the way he used to move in the jungle. He held up the long flame of a gas lighter. I dipped the cigarette down and puffed.

'Thanks, Ken.'

A click and the lighter disappeared. 'Tell me I'm looking well and I'll run this thing over your foot. It's heavy. It'll hurt.'

I said nothing. In fact, he didn't look good. He was pale and bloated in the face and flesh had built up on his torso. There was grey in his hair and moustache, and his eyes had sunk into puffy pouches. He wore an army shirt with no badges of rank. I couldn't help it; my eyes dropped to where his legs should have been. There was nothing. He'd been lopped off somewhere around mid-thigh.

'What happened, Ken?' I said.

He let out a short, barking sound that could have been a laugh, the way the twist of his mouth could have been a smile. 'That'd be right,' he said. 'Direct. No bullshit, eh, Hardy?'

'That's right.'

A man wearing an army shirt and trousers appeared with two schooners, handed one to Barraclough and one to me and disappeared into the crowd that was building up. Barraclough sank about half the schooner in a long gulp. 'Vietnam,' he said. 'Chance of a lifetime.'

I drank some of the beer. 'Mine?'

'Yeah. American mine.'

And that was the heart of the problem, right there. Barraclough told me that he'd been leading a patrol which had entered an area the Americans had mined without properly informing the Australian command. 'Bastards, lousy soldiers, gutless wonders. Could've done with you there, Hardy. But you'd had enough, right?'

'Right,' I said. I was leaning back against the wall, almost pinned there by the wheelchair. Barraclough's eyes glittered in their deep, soft sockets and his hands twitched nervously. Those hands, which I'd seen moving faster than the eye could follow—loading, firing, signalling—now seemed to have a neurotic, uncoordinated life of their own. He clenched his glass, emptied it. Another appeared.

'So what brings you here?' Barraclough said. 'Now that you're a prosperous civilian.'

'Lawrie Bean asked me to have a word with you.'

'That little shit! Why would you be having anything to do with him?'

'I'm an insurance investigator these days, Ken. But I also do a bit of this and that to make ends meet. I'm working for Bean, sort of.'

The wheelchair spun away. 'Then you can get the fuck out! Eddie!'

I took two steps towards the retreating wheelchair before the man who'd been supplying Barraclough with beer stopped me. He grabbed my shoulder and his grip told me everything I needed to know about him. He was strong, balanced and ready for action. A professional. He was also big and on his own turf. I knew how to get out of a grip like that and I did it. I finished my beer and tossed the schooner to him. The gesture took him by surprise. He caught the glass and I feinted the punch that would've flattened him.

I said, 'Thanks for the drink, Ken,' stepped around Eddie and left the bar.

Driving back to North Sydney, I discovered that I was in an evil mood. Barraclough had been an artist in his way, and what had happened to him was wrong. He should have survived intact, or gone out clean, instead of being so badly damaged in mind and body. I was convinced of the mind damage. The Digger Bar and the pseudo-uniforms were grotesque, a sick joke.

I took it out on Astrid. I was morose and drank too much that night and was unresponsive in bed. I tried to make amends in the morning, but only partly succeeded. She asked me what was wrong and I told her a little about it, but she didn't understand. I didn't understand it myself, but somehow I didn't want to see Barraclough running a bloodhouse masquerading as an army mess. It seemed a denial of everything he'd done in the past out of sense of duty and commitment. I rang Bean and told him I'd need a little time.

'Did you talk to him?'

'Yes. He's a sick man.'

'Thanks very much, Dr Casey. Did you make him see sense?'

'We didn't get that far. Look, it's complicated. If you want me to work on it, I will. But it's not just a matter of persuading Barraclough to take off the slouch hat.'

'Shit. The Yanks're due any day. All it'll take is for a couple of drunk GIs to go across the road and talk to those fuckin' ANZAC types Barraclough's got over there, and it'll be on! The cops'll close us both down. Who wins then?'

'Your thinking's too simple, Lawrie. He blames the US for what happened to him. He *wants* a stoush, he needs it.'

Bean swore a few times and then asked me what I had in mind. I told him I needed to find out some more about Barraclough and how he'd got into the state he was in. That got me a silence on the line.

'Lawrie?'

'Yeah? I didn't think I was hiring a fuckin' trick cyclist.'

'You were calling me Ben Casey a minute ago. How come you can't back off on this "all the way with LBJ" shit?'

'There's money in it.'

'Come on. When the fleet's in everyone makes money. You don't need the neon stars 'n' stripes to make a quid.'

Another silence, then Bean said, 'I've got an American backer. He's keen on the whole thing.'

'Without him you're in trouble?'

'I'm down the dunny.'

'Well then, you can see how complicated it is, too. Give me a few days, Lawrie.'

Bean agreed and I got busy. I hadn't kept up a lot of army contacts, didn't go to regimental dinners and such, but I knew a few people who knew a few more. After a morning spent mostly on the telephone, I finally got through to the doctor who'd treated Barraclough and sat on the committee that handled his discharge and disability settlement. He was Dr Stuart Henry, now a Reserves major.

'Very sad case, Mr Hardy,' the doctor said. 'A brilliant officer, totally dedicated, who made two bad mistakes.'

'What d'you mean, doctor?' I asked.

'He ignored or refused to believe an advice from US Command that a certain area was mined. That was mistake number one. It was an area he needed to pass through to accomplish *his* mission, no doubt about that. He could have got a key to the mine placement, but he didn't. Mistake two. Give him credit, he was up front when they went in. And he paid the penalty.'

I had to frame the next query carefully. There's nothing the army likes less than to have its judgments questioned. 'Doctor, you know Barraclough insists that he wasn't advised of the mines.'

'Absurd,' Henry snapped. 'The Americans' paperwork was immaculate.'

I could imagine the scene: Barraclough with

mud on his boots and in his hair, sweat patches under his arms, anxious to take some position that would afford relief to his men and others. A paper blizzard blowing into his tent and the muddy boots stamping on it.

'What would you say was his mental condition when he was discharged, doctor?'

Henry sighed. 'Mr Hardy, I'm only talking to you because people I trust tell me you're discreet.'

'That's right,' I said.

Another sigh. 'He was a grenade with the pin out—paranoid, depressive, deluded.'

'Did he get a big payout—compensation, anything like that?'

A snort of derision. 'No. A standard wounded-in-action allowance, calculated according to rank and years of service.'

I knew what that meant—medical bills taken care of for life, but life still to be lived on a tight budget as the cost of living went up. 'Thank you, doctor,' I said. 'One last question—did Captain Barraclough come from a wealthy background?'

'I thought you knew him.'

'I did, but as a soldier. The soldier takes over the man. I didn't know anything about him personally.'

'Captain Barraclough's father was a soldier settler who went broke and shot himself after his wife left him. He was raised in orphanages and educated in reform schools. He's a self-made man, Mr Hardy.'

Which left the question—where had Barra-clough got the money to operate the pub? I did some ringing around about that, too, but got no answers. As a next step, I arranged to meet Grant Evans, my main police contact, for a drink that evening. As soon as I'd put the phone down I realised that this meant another call to Astrid to explain another late arrival home. It didn't go over too well.

I met Grant in the Metropolitan and told him the story. We were drinking middies of old and smoking my Drum.

'What do you want me to do?' Grant said.

'Find out if there's someone dirty behind Barraclough. If there is, you can step in and prevent the bloodbath that's bound to happen.'

Grant looked at me oddly. We'd known each other since Police Boys' Club days in Maroubra. I'd been best man at his wedding. We'd been in Malaya, too, although not in the same Company. He knew Barraclough only by reputation, not from personal experience. Still, what I was proposing sounded like a low blow to an old comrade.

'I don't know, Cliff. What if he's on the up and up? What if he borrowed legitimate money to get the pub? You'd be shoving him over the edge.'

'The man's off his head. If he goes on with this thing there's bound to be trouble. He could end up on a manslaughter charge or something like that. Closing the pub'd be the least of his worries.'

'You're exaggerating,' Evans said.

'I've got a bad feeling about this, Grant. Just poke around a bit, will you?'

He said he would and we had a few more beers. Astrid's reception, when I got back to North Sydney, somewhere around 9.30, amorous and contrite, was icy.

For the next few days I did the routine things, got home in time for dinner and tried to mend the domestic fences. I was half-successful. Astrid accused me of being distracted and wanted to know what was going on. I tried to explain the ins and outs of the Barraclough case, but she didn't understand.

'This is 1967,' she said, 'not the 1940s. People are different. They've been to school longer. Those soldiers aren't going to take bayonets to each other.'

'They will,' I said, 'if the conditions are right. If they get fuelled up enough and egged on in the right way.'

'Well, you've done the right thing. You've alerted the police. They'll be on the lookout.'

'I haven't alerted the police, love. I've just had a private talk with Grant.'

'Won't he pass it on?'

'Not without talking to me first.'

Astrid smoked Benson & Hedges—filters in the gold pack. She lit one now and blew smoke at the ceiling. 'God,' she said, 'it's like a secret society. You ex-army types. You're no better than my father.'

'Was he ex-army? You've never told me.'

'No. He went to Lodge, all tricked out in a dinner suit and carrying a little bag. My mother hated it. After he died, they came around and took the bag away. You're like savages, you men, with your clubs and games.'

Grant phoned me the next day. 'First batch of GIs're due in today.'

'Great. I took a walk past the pub and the club this morning. It's all systems go, on both sides. Beer's half-price at the Digger Bar for Australian servicemen and Lawrie Bean's advertising a shot and a beer at prices you wouldn't believe. For Yanks, that is. Did you find anything out about Barraclough?'

'Not much. He's the licensee. The pub's not tied to a brewery. It's owned by a company named Australian Holdings which is one of a group of subsidiaries of something called the Pacific Investments Corporation.'

'Jesus, is that legal?'

'They tell me it's the business structure of the future.'

'Who tells you that—the fraud squad?'

'We've got nothing to act on, Cliff. The boys on the beat can keep an eye out, but they're going to have their hands pretty full anyway. It's worrying.'

Grant Evans was a busy man with a weight problem, a family he loved and ambitions which were being frustrated. He was dead straight and found a lot to worry him inside the New South Wales police force. I could hear real concern in his voice now and I pressed him to tell me what else he knew. He admitted that he'd gone into the Digger Bar himself the night before. He'd left his cop suit and manner in the office—he was an ex-serviceman and a drinker and he knew how to conduct himself. What he'd overheard had alarmed him.

'Barraclough's crazy,' he said. 'He *wants* to see American and Australian soldiers fighting. He says the Americans are the real enemy in Vietnam. Reckons all they've got is equipment, no brains, no plans and no guts.'

'What about the military police? Can't our people and the Yanks bung on a bit of protection?'

Evans sighed. 'I sniffed around on that. There's a problem. Sydney got to be the Rest and Recreation base after a fair bit of negotiating. Brisbane was well in the running, being closer, but the line was that there could be some racial problems up there with the black GIs. We're more cosmopolitan and sophisticated, see?'

'Yeah,' I said, 'and it wouldn't look good to start staking out the bars with MPs.'

'Right. Not on the first night. We'll have to wait and see how it shapes up, Cliff.'

I was edgy and hard to get along with at home that night. Astrid pretended not to notice and I pretended not to notice that she was pretending.

In the morning, I called in at the Rocky

Mountain Bar and saw the signs of what I feared—broken glass on the pavement, some damage to the neon sign. Two big potted palms, which had stood outside, had been snapped off. Soil from the pots had been spilled over the lobby carpet. I went in and found Lawrie Bean supervising a clean-up. Inside, there didn't seem to be much damage, except to Bean. His tight grey waves were ruffled, his eyes were red-rimmed and he looked as if he needed lots of sleep.

He lit a Rothmans and flicked the match at me. 'Thanks, Hardy. You did a great job. We had visitors last night, tanked to the gills.'

'How many?'

'Enough. There was a couple of big black Marine sergeants here, as it happened. They managed to keep a bit of order. But it's going to get worse. People are going to get hurt.'

'What do your backers say?'

Bean would've spat if he hadn't been standing on his new carpet. 'They tell me to handle it. They're insured to the hilt, so what the fuck? I tell them we'll get closed down and they say talk to the right people. They don't understand how things work in Sydney. Hey, where're you going?'

'To see Barraclough.' I went up the steps fast and almost knocked over a man who was standing at the top, looking down into the gloom and shaking his head.

He steadied himself against the wall and I turned towards him to apologise.

'Cliff Hardy,' he said. 'What the hell are you doing here?'

It was Rhys Thomas, a journalist I knew slightly and didn't want to know any better. He worked for one of the tabloids and had tried to do a feature on me before I convinced him otherwise.

'Having an early morning drink,' I said. 'How about you?'

'Just came down to take a look at something we're not allowed to write about. Didn't know there was an insurance angle, but.'

'There isn't,' I said. 'What d'you mean?'

Thomas was a pasty-faced, nocturnal snoop. To even see him in daylight was rare. To see him working was an event. He bared his yellow teeth in an ingratiating smile. 'Tit for tat?'

'No. You said "we're" not allowed to write about something. That means other people know what you know. I'll ask them.'

He offered me a Senior Service, which was about the only tailor-made cigarette I found hard to resist. I needed a smoke and I took it. I lit it myself, though.

'Look, Hardy,' Thomas said, 'there was a stoush here last night. I saw the tail end of it. Pretty bad. Filed a piece and it got spiked. You know why?'

I puffed smoke and shook my head.

'There's no trouble for GIs in our fair city. That's official. How does that sit with you?'

I shrugged. 'I'm not a crusader, Rhys. Neither are you, last I heard.'

'A couple of our boys got hurt pretty badly here. Hospital cases. Whisked away and nothing's being said. What about that?'

It got to me—a bunch of politicians and city plutocrats sitting down and declaring what was what while dopey young soldiers jabbed broken glasses at each other. I grabbed Rhys by the arm and dragged him across the street. 'Come with me,' I said. 'There's a story here all right. You just might be the man to tell it, if that's the way it works out.'

I could feel fear and resistance in Thomas' body as I hauled him over to the Macquarie. 'Hardy,' he said, 'I'm not sure . . .'

'Nothing's sure, Rhys,' I said, 'except that you're going to get a very thick ear unless you come with me.'

Barraclough was holding court in the Digger Bar. He had a full schooner in his fist and an empty one at his elbow. A couple of his semi-uniformed cronies were gathered round—bristling moustaches, tattooed forearms, beer-glazed eyes.

'Well, well,' Barraclough crowed, 'it's Lieutenant Hardy who got out when the getting out was good. Top of the morning, Cliff.'

He raised the full schooner. I got close enough to knock it out of his hand. The beer sloshed and spilled over Eddie who was in close attendance. Eddie growled and got to his feet.

'Sit down, Eddie,' Barraclough slurred. 'Man's some kind of cop. Probably got a gun. Got a gun, Hardy?'

'No,' I said. 'I wouldn't need a gun for Eddie or anyone else here. I don't understand you, Ken. Why're all these arse-lickers around? And where was Eddie last night? I hear the Marines put a couple of Australians in St Vincent's.'

'There'll be other nights,' Barraclough said.

I was so incensed by the stupidity of it all that I shoved one of the courtiers aside and pushed my face close up to Barraclough's red, sweaty kisser. 'I'm ashamed of you, Ken. You were a great officer, the best. You made a mistake and paid hard for it. Now you want to fight a little GI versus Aussie war right here in the Cross. Fuck you! What gives you the right to put blokes in hospital with broken jaws and carved-up faces?'

'I didn't make any mistakes.'

'The brass say you did. Prove that you didn't.'

Barraclough roared something incoherent and slammed his fists down on his fat stumps.

'Foaming at the mouth doesn't prove a thing,' I said.

Eddie and a couple of the other heavies looked restless. They were all battling hangovers and could turn mean at any moment. Rhys Thomas had backed into the shadows, but he was soaking up every word. Barraclough was the key to it all. The trick was to force something conciliatory, something reasonable out of him.

'What about it, Ken?' I taunted him. 'Want to Indian wrestle? You used to be good at that. I saw you break a guy's arm once in Singapore. The bone came through the skin. Remember? Want to arm wrestle to prove you were right? Prove the Yanks never told you the fucking mines were there? Prove you didn't blow your fucking legs off yourself?'

There was silence in the room. The night's smoke and beer fumes hung in the air like cobwebs. Sweat poured from Barraclough's face as he fought to control his anger. He looked around at the men lolling in chairs, slumped over tables and his lip curled. He sucked in a deep breath and his eyes came to focus on me. They bored in, tested me, the way he used to do back when he was about to issue orders about how to kill and survive. Suddenly, he was sober and deadly again.

'No, Cliff,' he said softly. 'I'm out of condition and you're still in shape. But I'll tell you what. You get that little prick Bean to find a Yank who can fight and we'll put an Aussie up against him. Unarmed combat with no holds barred.'

'What's the point?' I said.

'That'll settle it. Win, lose or draw, I won't look for trouble with the Yanks. We'll fraternise.'

'No provocation?' I said. 'No Yankees Go Home and half-price beer for Australians?'

'Right,' Barraclough said.

It seemed like a possible solution to a mess that was bound to grow messier otherwise. I couldn't see Bean having any objection. Bound to be a dirty fight, but one unarmed brawl was better than a hundred with broken bottles.

'I'll put it to Bean,' I said. 'Who's going to fight for you?'

Barraclough signalled for a drink. A schooner arrived and he took a small sip and wiped his moustache, very much the mess officer. 'You are, Cliff. Who else?'

Rhys Thomas was practically incoherent with delight.

'What a story,' he babbled. 'What a story.'

I'd done the deal with Bean. The fight was set for two nights away. My opponent was going to be one of the black Marine sergeants. Thomas had all the details. I bought him a drink in a pub in Victoria Street and gave him the bad news.

'No story, Rhys,' I said, 'not yet awhile.'

'Yeah, yeah. When the fight's over. I appreciate that. But even with the hush-hush on, they can't suppress this.'

'You're missing the point. *I'm* suppressing it. I just took you along for recording purposes. I don't want anything written about this.'

'Hardy!'

'Maybe one day.'

'That's not good enough.'

'It has to be. If you don't agree, I'll make sure you don't get to see the fight.'

'I suppose you could do that, but how're you going to stop me writing about it?'

I lowered my glass and looked at him.

'Jesus, Hardy. You can be an evil-looking bastard when you try.'

'I'm going to have to be more than evil-looking to get out of this in one piece.'

'Come on. It'll be a set-up, won't it?'

'You don't know Barraclough. He'll make sure it's not.'

I went through the motions for the rest of the day and then went back over the bridge. Things weren't any better on the home front. Astrid tried. She asked me how the Barraclough matter was going and I wasn't forthcoming. What could I do? Tell her I was going *mano e mano* against some Harlem streetfighter for the sake of something I wasn't even clear about myself?

On the day of the fight, Grant Evans called to tell me how quiet it had been the night before. 'False alarm, eh, Cliff?'

I grunted.

'What's wrong?'

'Nothing. Sorry, Grant, I've got a few things on.'

He hung up, offended. Terrific. Just the way to go into a fight, with your woman cold and resentful and your best mate pissed off. I got through the day somehow. Astrid had told me that she wouldn't be in until nine. I said we could watch *Peter Gunn* together at 10.30. She wasn't amused.

I turned up at the Macquarie at 9.00 p.m. wearing jeans, tennis shoes and an old army shirt. I leaned against a car outside and waited until Barraclough came to me. A couple of his boys had lifted the wheelchair up to street level and were looking a bit distressed. Barraclough was drunk.

'Where?' I said.

'Out the back. That little prick of a journalist reckons you said he could watch. That right?'

'Yeah. I hope you haven't sold tickets.'

Barraclough chuckled. 'Just a few friends, Hardy. Just a few friends.'

The wheelchair had an electric motor. He drove it along a narrow lane beside the pub and through a gate into a small yard, floodlit from the wooden stairs that led down from the back of the hotel. It looked as if Barraclough's backers planned some improvements out here. The cement had been taken up and the yard was about to be bricked. The bricks, nice ones, salvaged from some de-molished building, were in stacks around the edge. The space, about the size of two boxing rings, was covered with a couple of inches of sand. Lawrie Bean was there, along with three men in US military uniform, three Australian soldiers and Rhys Thomas. A woman sat on the bricks, smoking. Along with Barraclough, me and Eddie, that made twelve. The woman came across to stand beside Barraclough's wheelchair. She was a leggy blonde with a miniskirt, sequined top and a face hard enough to knock the mortar off the old bricks.

A man stepped from the shadows near the steps.
Number thirteen. He wore fatigue pants, a singlet
and basketball boots. He was about six-foot-two,
fourteen stone and black. Except for his teeth.
They were very white when he smiled, which he
did now.

'Hi, honky,' he said. 'I understand you don't
like niggers.'

I shot a told-you-so look at Thomas but I didn't
bother to reply. I took off my watch, removed
the money from my pockets and put the lot on
the bricks, never taking my eyes off the Marine.
He spat on his hands and dropped into a crouch.

'Sergeant Lester Dobbs,' he said. 'Whose ass do
I have the pleasure of whipping?'

'My name's Hardy,' I said, 'and you talk too
bloody much.'

He scooped up a handful of sand and whipped
it at me, but I was ready for that and went in
under it with my eyes slitted. I kicked for his
groin; he shuffled fast and took it on the thigh.
My foot bounced off rock-hard muscle. He came
at me, jabbing out a left, right cocked, balanced.
I moved my head enough to avoid the jab and
hit him on the nose with a quick one of my own.
Too light, rusty, not enough snap. He got me with
the right below my left eye and I went down.
I saw his huge blue and white basketball boot
coming for my ribs and twisted away; he missed,
lost balance momentarily and I swept his feet from
under him with a scythe kick. Even falling, he

was fighting; he came down hard on top of me and we grappled in the sand, kicking and clawing until I got away, courtesy of one good elbow to his ear.

We were up again, circling. I could feel blood on my face and there was a roaring in my ears. He was sweating and dirty but unmarked, smiling. I didn't even see the roundhouse right that caught me in exactly the same place as the first one and closed my eye. I claimed him and brought my knee up which hurt him a bit but not enough to stop him butting me. I felt my nose break, not for the first time, and pain spread through my skull. I might have landed a few more times, I don't remember. All that stays with me is the hiss and stink of his boozy breath as he hit me, left and right, head and body. The pain was everywhere, mounting to a crescendo. I felt a tooth collapse, then my mouth was full of sand and the pain stopped.

I heard Dobbs say, 'Guy can fight.' Then I was lifted up and propped against the bricks. Something damp was passed across my face and a glass was lifted to my mouth. I sucked in beer, choked and sprayed it out with blood and the broken tooth.

'Jesus, Hardy.'

I recognised Rhys Thomas' voice but I couldn't see him. My left eye was closed and the other had sand in it. I lifted my hand to rub the good eye and felt the blood dripping from my knuckles.

I smiled. I thought, *Must've landed one punch at least.*

'He's laughing,' Thomas said.

Barraclough sounded almost sober. 'Hardy's got some fuckin' funny ideas, but he's not a squib.'

I said, 'I don't hate niggers.'

Dobbs' ripe breath was close to my face again. 'Say what?'

I had just enough strength to raise my hand and wiggle the fingers. 'Joe Louis was the greatest fighter and Louis Armstrong's the greatest horn player ever.'

'An' the best singer?' Dobbs said.

'Ella Fitzgerald,' I said.

'You're all right, man. Who's going to take this guy home?'

I don't know how it happened, but the next thing I knew I was sitting in the back seat of my Falcon. My shirt was ripped but I could feel my watch and money in the pocket. Dobbs was driving and the blonde in the miniskirt was sitting next to me soaking up my blood with tissues. We crossed the bridge.

'Walker Street,' she said. 'Turn here, sweetie.' She had a nice, soft, breathy Sydney voice.

Then we were on the landing outside the flat and the woman was ringing the bell and Dobbs was holding me up.

Astrid opened the door. She was wearing one of her black silk nighties and looked adorable.

Her eyes went wide at the sight of the Negro, the battered bloody ruin and the whore.

'Christ,' she said. 'Is it always going to be like this?'